DISCOMBOBULATED

A Novel By
Steven Morgan

Second Edition: May 2015

ISBN-13: 9781512016918
ISBN-10: 1512016918

Published by:
KingPen Enterprises
Chicago, IL

Acknowledgements

First and foremost, I would like to thank GOD for everything. Without him none of this would be possible, but with him in my life everything is possible. I love you.

I want to give a special thanks to Shana, for the support you give me everyday. No matter what, I know you'll love me the same if I sold one or 1 million books. Thank you for being such a lovely person.

To my daughters, Amari, Anyah, and Aubrey, Daddy loves you more than life itself. You're my motivation, and I'll die trying to give you the world. Every time I look at one of you, I just want to work harder. Thank you, God, for blessing me with three angels.

I would like to thank my parents, Diana and Robert, for their love and support. Mom, thank you for always being there for me. I love you. I want to thank my brother, Bobby, for his support and direction. Much love to you, big bro. I would like to thank all of my family and friends that supported me through this hard journey. Thank you Oddball Designs for the book cover. You're the best in the business! Thanks to everyone behind the scenes that helped during this process. To anyone that I've missed, I am truly sorry. You know that I appreciate you. Lastly, I would like to ask God to continue to bless and protect everyone on earth.

Until next time... Steven Morgan.

Prologue

Karma, baby!

You either live life passionately or die tragically, and I don't plan on dying anytime soon. I can't even remember how I got myself into this situation. It doesn't really matter anymore, does it? I'm here now, so I have to do what is necessary. That was my problem. My entire existence I've been going through life taking shit from my husband, my best friend, and even my damn momma. May God bless all of their wonderful souls, but let me tell you something. Their souls were not wonderful to me. I just have respect for them and decided to put away the grudges. I put up with all of their drama and never did anything about it. Then, something must have snapped in my mind. I wasn't going to play the fool anymore. I will always have a place for them in my heart, but it was due time for me to move on. Maybe that's why I am where I am today. I waited too long to take control of my life, and now I'm playing catch up. And believe what I tell you. Baby, I am catching up. From here on out, it's all about me.

Who am I, you ask? My name is Ciara Blackwell, and I am here to tell you that all Black women are not angry. Some of us were just so mistreated that we had to learn how to live again, even if that meant putting a couple of fools in their place from time to time. So, to all the dirty dick muthafuckers, conniving- ass females, and those playing straight when you're really gay niggas and taking advantage of the weak…before you use your one-way ticket to hell, maybe you should all line up and kiss my round, plump, black ass! And to everyone out there like me, take back your power before it's too late and you end up like me. My life is discombobulated, and I don't wish my condition on my worst enemy.

Chapter 1

"It's four o'clock in the damn morning, and he hasn't called or came in yet," Ciara mumbled as she glanced at the clock on the nightstand.

Another Saturday night and Ciara had spent it home alone waiting for her husband to come in from a night of supposedly kicking it. Once she adjusted her eyes to the dark room, she searched for her cell phone and located it, but not before knocking over a glass of Absolut Vodka. Immediately, she dialed Shawn's number and waited.

"This ya boy Shawn. Leave a message and I'll return your call."

To Ciara's surprise, her call had been sent straight to his voicemail. She smacked her lips, then jumped out of bed and started pacing the floor. She began hollering into the phone as if Shawn was actually on the other end.

"Shawn, do you know what time it is? No, you don't. I'm getting worried about you! Call me back, you selfish bastard! No, better yet, bring your black ass home! I hope that piece of ass is worth it, because you might meet your maker today!"

Ciara hung the phone up in a rage. She couldn't believe Shawn was on his same bullshit again.

Discombobulated

"He must think I'm a damn fool!" She screamed, as she almost tripped over a pair of four-inch stilettos that were on the floor.

Ciara decided Shawn's nonchalant ways had to come to an end. After tossing her phone on the foot of the bed, she grabbed a box of cigarillos that were on the nightstand next to the clock.

If his ass isn't here by the time I finish rolling this blunt, it's going to be on, she thought.

Ciara sat on the edge of the bed, and using the illumination from the digital clock, she slowly began to break down the Swisher, hoping Shawn would come in before she finished rolling up. She crumbled the light green dro into the peach cigar carefully, trying not to drop any of the dank. She then placed the cigar in between her lips and began to apply enough saliva to seal the blunt completely across.

"I'm going to smoke half of this, and if his ass isn't in this house by then, I'm going out on the hunt."

Ciara lit the blunt and started her session. As the smoke built up in her chest from the heavy tokes of the bud, all she could think about was Shawn banging another chick. After all the bullshit she had to deal with, he still treated her like a bitch on the side.

I bet he got his ass a white girl this time.

The reason for Ciara's thought was because lately, every word she said, Shawn tried to correct her as if he was a damn English teacher.

It took no time before Ciara finished smoking the tightly rolled blunt and was starting on her next one. The room was cloudy like a smoke bomb had gone off. The heavy stench of marijuana eliminated the cool air caused from the air conditioner. She took another hit of the weed and placed the blunt on the ashtray by her side. By then, she was on a level only smokers could relate to.

An hour later, after realizing she was still waiting for Shawn to come in, Ciara snatched up her cell phone and car keys and raced out of the door. As soon as she got into her black on black Nissan Altima, she turned on the wipers and the rear defroster to clear the foggy windows. She reached over and grabbed her Sidekick off of the passenger seat, but she was so high and upset, that she forgot who she was about to call. Once she took a deep breath and managed to calm herself a little, she remembered she was about to call Kim, her partner in crime. Even though Kim had just left Ciara's house hours ago after they crushed a fifth of Absolut mixed with cranberry juice, Ciara needed her.

"Hello," a groggy voice on the other end answered.

"I know you're sleep, Kim, but I have to talk to you right now."

"What? Who is this?" Kim asked in her half-sleep and hung-over state.

"It's me, Ciara!"

"Ciara Blackwell? What time is it, girl?"

"I know it's late, but I needed to talk to you."

"What's the matter? Did you try to stab Shawn again?" Kim asked, while sitting up in her bed. "Tell me, girl. My head hurts and I don't have time for the guessing games."

"No, I haven't stabbed him, but this fool hasn't made it home yet. This time I know he's out with another chick! I just know he is, Kim! I can feel it!" Ciara said, as she closed her eyes for a brief second, trying not to think about Shawn being with another female.

"Why do you always jump to conclusions like that?" Kim asked, while tightening her loosened hair scarf.

Hurt and embarrassed by Shawn's actions, tears began to flow down Ciara's face. "Kim, it's almost six o'clock in the morning. The club closes at three, so what can be taking him so long to get home?"

Kim had been through this routine with Ciara time and time again, but she was Ciara's best friend and had her back no matter what happened.

"First of all, stop crying like a damn baby and calm down. You're starting to sound like his mother."

Ciara screamed in the phone, "Mother, my ass! Put some clothes on. We're about to go and find him and the bitch that he's with!"

"Listen here, girl. I'm not getting involved with you and Shawn's mess again. Besides, it's too early for all this nonsense."

"I don't give a damn if the world is about to come to an end! I need to find out what's going on!"

There was a long pause on the phone.

"Are you high?" Kim asked, breaking the silence. "I told you to stop buying Greg's weed. That shit has you on another planet when you smoke it."

"Yes, I'm high, but I can still function."

Kim climbed out of bed, turned on the light, and began getting dressed.

"This is insane, Ciara. Still, I'll be ready in twenty minutes."

Ciara smiled because she knew Kim would be down for her no matter what.

"Make it five minutes, 'cause I'm already on my way over there. That ass is mine when I see him," she said before ending the call.

CLICK!

"I know this hoe didn't hang up on me," Kim said, while staring down at the phone in her hand.

Accustomed to the routine, Kim quickly finished putting on her clothes. This was not the first time they had to take care of some spur-of-the-moment business, and it probably wouldn't be the last time.

Ciara Blackwell and Kimberly Morris had been best friends since the seventh grade, which was around the time Ciara's father Jarvis left the family and moved to Tampa Bay, Florida with a white girl named Stacey. Since that day, Ciara and her mother carried a dislike toward white women.

Loretta, Ciara's mother, use to call her Always-on-Her-Knees Stacey. Loretta believed that Jarvis left her because he got used to the oral services Stacey gave to him daily. She failed to mention all the shit he had to deal with during their thirteen-year relationship. Like the time when Jarvis came home from working a double shift and found another man's wallet in between the cushions of the couch. Ciara thought her father was going to catch a case that night from the way he was beating on Loretta.

Ciara's mother always had a nonchalant attitude about life, but reality hit home when Jarvis left. The money was limited and the hard times came rolling in like a runaway train. There were times when Ciara and her mother had to take cold showers because the gas had been turned off. It was far from Kanye West's version of a "Good Life".

Ciara experienced a lot of hungry, lonely nights. Working two jobs, Loretta didn't have time for her daughter. She worked first shift at the local grocery store and second shift every night at the kitchen table with a fifth of Jack Daniels. Ciara didn't have a choice but to turn to Kim and the streets.

Ciara and Kim were both loved and hated by many on the Westside of Chicago. They also were notorious for beating down chicks on the regular. Whether it was over money or a boy, the duo had always taken care of their business accordingly. Some of the local chicks tried them, but not many.

Ciara learned from Kim, and Kim learned from Ciara. As time went on, Ciara calmed down a lot, but it was always in her to be ghetto when she needed to be. Growing up in Chicago brought out the best and worst in both of them.

Discombobulated

The summer before Ciara left for college, her mother died from a rare liver disease. Ciara knew her mother was going to drink herself into an early grave, but she didn't expect it to happen so soon. After her mother's death, she decided to communicate only with Kim because her other family was a little too dysfunctional. Ciara had an uncle named Marion that was in and out of prison. He did a six-year bid for robbery when Ciara was only three years old. He did another twelve years for kidnapping and sexual assault after his first six-year bid. Another crazy relative of Ciara's was her older cousin Ronald, who was on the Jarvis side of the family. He had a sex change three days before Loretta's funeral. It was more attention on Ronald, or shall we say Rolanda, than it was on Loretta's death.

The death of her mother slowed her down tremendously. Still, she focused on life itself. She wasn't the working type, but she worked overtime making sure her husband Shawn was taken care of.

On a scale from one to ten, Ciara was considered a dime. At 5'4" and 132 pounds, she was the perfect fit for most men; with her caramel complexion and long, jet-black, shoulder-length hair that was all her own and not store bought. With light brown eyes and a million dollar smile, she had an innocent, but sexy look. She was like the teacher that every boy had a crush on in school, but sexier. On her bad days, Ciara still looked better than half of the females on the block. The hustlers always wanted a piece of her. A day didn't go by without somebody trying to buy their way into her pants. She even had the lesbians after her. You name it and Ciara was offered it, from Chinchilla coats to wedding rings. She had heard every line written in the *Chicago Player's* handbook.

One hustler named Macho always gave Ciara money whenever he saw her. He called her his "future wifey" and would always check any nigga on the block that tried to disrespect her. But, by the time Ciara started to have feelings for

Macho, he got caught with nine bricks of dope and was hit with thirty years of federal time. So, that "bust it baby" relationship was over before it even started.

Ciara could have men lined up waiting to serve her if she wanted. She was the type of woman that could have her cake and eat it, too. However, she was too in love with Shawn to notice most of the men that approached her, which was something Kim couldn't understand about Ciara.

Kimberly Morris was the total opposite of her best friend. Not a lot had changed about Kim, except for the year. She had been the same since they were kids. She didn't have much family like Ciara, and the family she had, most of them were strung out on drugs. Her mother was a heavy drug user, and her father had been out of the picture since the day her mother told him she was pregnant. He said he was going to the store to get cigarettes, but neither he nor the cigarettes made it back home. About six years later, her mother died on Christmas Eve from a drug overdose. From that day on, Kim sought love and security from the boys and men she came across in the streets.

Kim used her looks and body for bait, just like she did when she was fourteen by getting older men on the block to buy beer and wine coolers for her. Since then, Kim had been around the block a couple of times. Better yet, Kim had been around a couple of blocks, a couple of times. She only dealt with breadwinners. Men had to have money or she advised them not to walk on the same side of the street as her. She didn't discriminate either. You could be a drug dealer, doctor, preacher, or whatever. As long as you had it, she had to have it.

A redbone with a ghetto-fabulous physique, Kim stood about 5'4", weighed 135 pounds that was mostly breast and ass, sported a different hair color every month, and wore hazel contacts that she claimed to be her original eye color. Kim didn't have a job, but she continuously wore the latest designer clothes. Ms. Morris didn't shy away from the competition

Discombobulated
either. She was a true competitor when it came to men. She stayed on her "A" game and was never afraid to take another woman's man. Being the bold woman that she was, she even tried to get Shawn from Ciara on the low.

******

Kim tried to brace herself in the passenger seat.

"Slow down a little bit. You're making me nervous as hell over here!" Kim said, as she quickly fastened her seatbelt.

"I'm sorry. I just can't understand why this man is trying to play me again. Another female after everything I've done for him?" Ciara said in a low voice.

"So you know for a fact that he's with another woman?"

"What? Are you serious?" Ciara replied, glancing over at her. She couldn't believe the words that came out of her mouth.

"Yes, I'm serious. You can't just accuse the brother when he hasn't given you a reason to."

"This is the third weekend in a row that he's left me in that damn house, claiming that he's going out with Eric and those fools from his job."

"What a man, what a man!" Kim repeated, as she fanned herself and shook her head repeatedly.

"What's wrong?" Ciara asked.

"Nothing, just had a quick flashback."

"You're nasty as hell, Kim. Don't be over there thinking about you and Eric's mini fuckfest."

"I'm sorry. I'm here with you, girl." Kim wiped a bead of sweat from her forehead as she thought of Eric. "Look, if Shawn hasn't given you a reason to believe he's cheating, you shouldn't be tripping like this. That's all I'm saying."

"I just hate it when he lies to me. He told me that he was going to have a couple of drinks with Eric, so I called him to see if he was alright."

"Okay, and what did he say when he answered the phone?" Kim asked, noticing the anguish building up in Ciara by the way she gripped the steering wheel tighter.

"Nothing, because as soon as he answered, he must have noticed it was me and hung up."

"Damn, girl! Yeah, he's getting his juke on for sure," Kim replied, then reclined back in her seat.

"Do you know where they go after the club?"

"No!" Kim quickly answered.

"Stop lying, bitch, because that's where you hooked up with Eric at."

"Why are you all in my business, Ciara?"

"Anyway. Where did they go?" Ciara waved her hand at Kim, dismissing her comment.

"They usually go to the IHOP off of North Avenue."

"Well, it's time for a U-turn, baby, because that's our next stop."

Ciara turned the steering wheel quickly to the left, avoiding a pothole. Twenty minutes later, they were pulling into the parking lot of the IHOP where Ciara assumed Shawn would be.

"Is that Eric's car right there?" Ciara asked, as she slowly pulled up next to Eric's Aurora.

"If 'E-Luv' is on the plates, that's it."

Ciara noticed Eric's specialized plates. Therefore, she got out of the car.

"Come on. Let's go in!"

"Hell no! I can't go in there looking like a broke down hoe in front of Eric."

"Trust me, you would still look like a broke-down hoe if you were fresh out of Beyoncé's camp."

"You got your nerve!"

Kim walked slowly behind Ciara, reluctant to go in. She tried her best to fix her tangled ponytail before anyone else saw

Discombobulated

her.

"Come on!" Ciara pulled Kim by the arm across the lot. After swinging open the door to the restaurant and entering, she spotted Shawn sitting in a corner booth.

"There go his black ass right there," Ciara said, pointing her index finger in Shawn's direction.

He was leaned back into the booth while puffing on a Black and Mild cigar. He hadn't noticed Ciara and Kim walking in his direction. It didn't matter, though, because Shawn's calm demeanor wouldn't allow him to be embarrassed by Ciara's fanatical behavior.

Shawn Blackwell was a smooth brother from Carbondale, Illinois. He was about 6'2", 215 pounds, and had dark skin, light brown eyes, and a low, neatly-trimmed afro and goatee. His brother Eric called him "the dark-skinned Will Smith". He had an athletic frame, and all the credit was due to his wrestling days at Northern Illinois University. Shawn worked as a general manager at Footlocker and also as an event promoter in the Chicagoland area along with Eric.

Besides promoting events, his brother Eric worked as a paramedic with the city of Chicago. Eric was about 6'1", 170 pounds, brown skinned, had a low haircut, goatee, and one gold tooth in his mouth. Eric was the younger of the two and the baby of the family, as well. Shawn and Eric had an older brother that was a police officer, but he had been killed in the line of duty when Shawn and Eric were still in high school.

"What's wrong with you, Shawn?" Ciara yelled out.

"What's wrong with me?" Shawn asked in a shocking voice, as he dropped his Black and Mild on the table. "What's wrong with you, Ciara? Why are you in here like this? This doesn't make any sense."

Shawn placed his cigar in the ashtray with force.

"You don't even have any clothes on, Ciara! You're out here in some holey pajamas and a bogus, early-morning, bus-stop house robe!"

"Don't worry about that! Where the hell is that white bitch?" Ciara yelled, looking around the restaurant.

"Where is who? What are you talking about?" Shawn looked deeply into her red eyes. "You're high, aren't you? I told your ass to stop smoking so much weed!"

At that point, Shawn couldn't do anything but shake his head at Ciara's behavior.

"Shawn, I was born at night, but not last night!"

Eric turned his head and began to laugh.

"I'm glad this shit is funny to you, Eric, but when that hoe comes out of the bathroom, I'm going to laugh on her pale ass!"

"Calm down!" Shawn placed a twenty-dollar bill on the table and looked to Eric so they could haul ass out of there.

"Twenty dollars? How many people are you paying for, Shawn?"

"Relax, woman! Eric didn't have any cash on him, so I'm paying for his meal."

Kim stood there not saying a word. She was too focused on how good Eric was looking in his Sean John outfit.

"Hey, Eric," Kim finally said, as she wasted no time dropping her eyes to his crotch.

"What's up, sexy?"

"What happened to my phone call, E?" Kim folded her arms, standing in a sexy-ass stance.

"I forgot to call you. I had to handle some business out of town. You know how it is."

"Eric, please don't give me that. You were supposed to call me two weeks ago."

"I was, but…"

Before he could finish his sentence, Kim cut him off. "Don't even worry about it."

"I'm sorry. It's not like that, baby girl. What are you doing

Discombobulated when you leave here?" Eric asked with a seductive smile, exposing his gold tooth.

"Taking her ass home!" Ciara butted in, snapping her fingers.

"Ciara, I can talk for myself. Thank you very much," Kim fired back, then turned to Eric again. "Why? You want to give me a ride home?"

Eric stood and placed his arm around Kim's shoulder. "Yeah, come on. I want to holla at you about something anyhow."

Shawn stood up from the table with his hands outstretched. "What about me? I know you're just not going to leave me after I've paid for your food?"

"Man, you're cool. Your wife is standing right there."

"No, if he doesn't start talking, his ass will be hitchhiking tonight, Eric."

"Ciara, can we talk in the car?" Shawn asked in a low voice, trying to keep her under control and everybody else out of their business.

"Whatever, let's go! What the hell are y'all looking at?" Ciara yelled, as she and Shawn walked by a couple that were waiting to be seated.

Shawn slowly followed Ciara back to her car that was parked in a handicap spot near the door. On the way home, he tried his best to remain silent.

"So when are you going to start talking, Shawn?"

He didn't respond.

"I knew it. I knew you were with someone."

"No, that's where you're wrong. I wasn't with another woman, Ciara."

"Well, I hope it wasn't another man!"

"You know I don't even get down like that, so don't play with me."

"So where were you? And before you lie, I know you were

at the club because I heard the music playing in the background before you hung up in my ear."

"Okay, I was at the club," he reluctantly answered.

"That's all you had to say. You didn't have to sneak and go to the club with Eric. I would've understood. I thought we could talk about things like that?"

"I wasn't just at the club. I was at the strip club," he shamefully admitted.

Ciara's heart began to race. At the beginning of their marriage, Shawn was addicted to strip clubs, which caused major problems in their relationship because he spent so much time and money there.

"Don't tell me you started that shit again."

As he sat quietly, Ciara could only shake her head in disbelief while waiting for a response from her husband.

"I've been going for the last three weeks, Ciara."

She suddenly slammed on the brakes.

"What! I can't believe this! You're taking our money and giving it to some fake-ass Ronnie and Tricks at the strip club!"

"No, it's not like that."

"Well, what is it like, Shawn?"

"Let me explain, baby, but you can't get mad at me when I tell you what happened. You have to just hear me out."

"Talk, Shawn. I'm all ears," she replied, her eyes blurry from the tears that had formed.

"Last month when we had the birthday party for Eric, I met this woman. She was one of the performers. And she just blew my mind with the things she was doing on stage."

"So you're in love with a stripper bitch like you're T- Pain or somebody?"

"Please, let me explain, Ciara. I don't love her, but she…" He paused, unable to finish his sentence.

"She what, Shawn?" Ciara screamed, ready to explode inside.

"She treats me different. A lot different than you do."

"Oh, she treats you different? And how does she treat you different than I do? Wait! I know. I only see your money, but she takes it from you? Now I get it!"

"She respects me as a man!"

"What? I should fuck you up! Are you really telling me this?"

"You just don't get it."

"Get off that soap opera shit and tell me the truth! We're talking about a stripper! How much respect can she give you?" Ciara pulled into their driveway and slammed the car into park.

Shawn could only stare at her.

"So what do we need to do about this?"

"I love you and I'll always love you, but…"

"But what?" Ciara asked. Although, she truthfully didn't want to hear anything else he had to say.

"I think we should see other people," Shawn suggested. He had to turn away from her gaze because he didn't have the nerve to say it while looking at her expression. "You know, an open marriage."

"Let's see. Since we're married, that means we're getting a divorce?"

Shawn could hear the hurt and pain in Ciara's voice.

"No, I'm not saying that."

"So what in the hell are you saying then?"

"I think we should have an open relationship."

"Open relationship? No, either we're together or we're not. I don't believe in having an open relationship."

Shawn didn't know what to say, because inside, he still wanted to be with his wife. However, he also wanted to be with his newfound love.

Ciara's eyes filled with tears as she looked at him. She was a second away from popping him on the side of his head, but instead, she banged on the steering wheel to let out some of the frustration.

"I just have to be real with myself, Ciara, and I have done you wrong too many times just to keep lying and hurting you."

He reached into his pocket, grabbed his keys, and slowly stepped out of the car.

"Hold on, motherfucker! This shit isn't over! Bring your ass here now!" Ciara jumped out of the car and ran towards Shawn as he opened the front door. "You have me in this fucking house all the time while you're out with another hoe!"

"I'm not trying to do this tonight. See, that's why I don't come home, 'cause you be on some other shit!"

"You're supposed to talk to me about everything. What happened to talking?"

"I don't want to talk about this anymore," Shawn replied, as if that was it.

"You're about to tell me something, or I'm about to knock these fucking walls down tonight!"

"See, that's the dumb shit I'm talking about. I don't have to go through this shit with you, Ciara," he said, while walking into the house.

"What? Oh yeah?" Ciara screamed, rushing past him towards the kitchen.

"Fuck this. I'm gone." Shawn turned around and left back out the door, not waiting around to see if he would end up stabbed or shot.

By the time Ciara made it to the front door, he was in his car and down the street.

I can't believe this. I can't believe Shawn would do me like this.

Ciara closed the door and dropped to her knees. A lump formed in her throat and a knot landed in the pit of her stomach. Her body felt numb. She looked around her, as if someone else was present. The house was quiet except for the humming of the fish tank's filter as tears fell from Ciara's face. It was a lot for

Discombobulated

her to swallow.

Chapter 2

"Man, I can't believe you broke it down to Ciara like that? I didn't know that stripper had you tripping like this. I could see if she had some good pussy or something, but you said she was weak in bed," Eric said to Shawn.

"I just had to be real about the whole situation. Besides, it's about time I started telling Ciara the truth," Shawn replied.

"So what do you think Ciara's next step will be?"

"I really don't know, but I'm going to go and look for an apartment in the morning. Just in case Pink be on some bullshit, I'll at least have somewhere to rest my head. Eric, if I would've stayed there last night, Ciara would've tried to kill me. Man, I don't know what she was going for when she ran into the kitchen."

"Oh, she was getting something for that ass, bro!"

Shawn laughed because he knew it was true.

"I have to steal a page from your player's handbook. You have a nice setup, big bro. A girlfriend and a wife on the side!"

"Yeah, but it's a different feeling. Something I just can't explain. I love Ciara, but I also have feelings for Pink."

Shawn exhaled, pondering on his move and his motives.

"So let me get this straight. You told Ciara that you wanted to have an open relationship, right?"

"Yeah, and what's the big deal?" Shawn replied.

"Now, follow me on this one. If Ciara finds herself a male friend, and let's just say his name is Johnny Longstroke. Are you willing to accept the friendship she has with Mr. Longstroke, even if it's just a physical relationship?" Eric asked, then pressed his ear closer to the phone so he could hear everything Shawn had to say in response.

"If it comes to that, I just have to respect the rules of the open relationship."

"I don't believe you. You're talking crazy, Shawn. You and I both know that if she started sleeping with another dude, you're going to go crazy. You can save all that 'respect the rules of the open relationship' bullshit for somebody else!" Eric mocked Shawn's voice.

"I'll put it like this. I know my woman. As long as we're in some type of relationship, she isn't going to let nobody else have that. I broke her in, and I'm the one who turned her out. So, it's going to take some time before she lets somebody else trespass on my property."

"Okay, I'll take your word for it, but you're playing with fire. You've seen *The Best Man*, right? Did you see how Morris Chestnut was looking? He needed a 'get well soon' card because he was sick when he thought about his girl getting hit. That chick was biting the covers and moaning. I don't think you can handle that. So, yeah, you're playing with fire, Shawn."

"I got this under control. Who do you think taught you this game?" At this point, Shawn was full of too much confidence. "I'll talk to you later, E. I'm about to grab Pink something to eat from T.G.I. Friday's."

"Okay, but do me a favor."

"What? I know you're not about to tell me anything about my women again?"

"Think about what you're doing. I know you made your mind up already, but just give it some more time before you make your final decision. I think you're moving too fast with the stripper chick."

"Yeah, whatever you say, E, and stop calling her that. Her name is Pink."

Eric knew Shawn was falling too fast for Pink because of the comment he just made.

"I just don't want you to make a long-term decision because of some short-term bullshit."

"Eric, trust me, I got this under control. I never put myself into situations I can't handle. I'll talk to you later."

After Shawn hung up, Eric just shook his head as he stood up from his dining room table.

******

"Hold on for one second, Ciara. I have to switch phones."

Kim placed Ciara on hold while she grabbed the other cordless phone from her bedroom.

"Okay, I'm back, but that nigga is tripping, Ciara. What's wrong with him? You don't deserve that from him or any nigga for that matter. If he wants to date other people, don't stop him, because that's what he wants and he's going to do whatever he wants to do anyway. That's how these dummies get down out here. They always think with the wrong head."

"But that's not what I want. I blame myself for everything. I became lazy and comfortable with my husband. I stopped being the woman he fell in love with. I forgot my place in my marriage. I wasn't taking care of my man."

Kim could hear the resentment in Ciara's voice.

"I know, but you can't hold him back because it's going to make the situation worse. We both know you were going to kill Shawn if he had stayed in that house with you last night. To be honest, Ciara, I would've left your crazy ass in the house last night, too."

"I'm not crazy. I'm just so in love with him, and I don't know what else to do."

The sound of desperation in her friend's voice tugged at her heart, and Kim knew she had to do something to make her girl feel better.

"How about we go out for dinner tonight, then go out and have us some drinks on me?"

"On you?" Ciara asked, surprised.

"Yeah, I got some money to play with."

"Hold on, Kim. I don't mean to change the subject, but did you sleep with Eric last night?"

"No, I just offered my professional services to him in exchange for some cash."

"Professional bust-down services," Ciara said, while laughing into the receiver.

"Whatever. I don't look at it like that. I look at it on a professional level. I'm a call girl."

"Yeah, a booty-call girl. I thought Eric didn't have any money last night since Shawn paid for his food?"

"Girl, you know I'm a hustler. I made that fool go to the ATM at five o'clock in the morning for some of this good yellow ass."

"I guess you're a professional hoe then."

"Whatever. I'll talk to you later, girl."

After hanging up, Shawn still remained on Ciara's mind as she glanced at his name that was tattooed on her leg.

Many thoughts ran through her mind.

This feels like a sick, confusing dream. It's not like he was drunk and didn't know what he was saying, because he said the same thing this morning when I called him. I need to get some fresh air. Maybe I'll go work out at the gym today. I should make Kim take her ass with me.

Ciara pressed redial on her phone, and after two rings, Kim answered.

"Yes, Mrs. Blackwell, how may I help you?"

"Hey, do you want to go to the gym for a couple of hours?"

"Ciara, you don't even know where a gym is! So, how in the hell are we going to go to the gym? Besides, I already had my workout for the day."

"You are so nasty! I can't believe you fuck with Eric like that."

"What? You act like he got six different baby mommas or something."

"Damn near!" Ciara replied. "He's already got three. Are you trying to be baby momma number four?"

"Whatever, Ciara. Don't hate on me because I brought sexy back. Hello! Are you still there?"

The next thing Kim heard was a dial tone in her ear.

"I know this trick didn't hang up on me," she said, while staring at the phone in disbelief.

******

"I need to do something before I start thinking about Shawn again."

Ciara's train of thought was cut short when she heard someone coming through the front door.

"Speaking of the devil. Now he wants to bring his ass

home."

"Ciara! Ciara!" he yelled from the bottom of the stairs in his deep voice.

"What do you want?" she replied with a raised voice.

"I'm going to look at an apartment in the morning, and I'll let you know when I'll be officially moved out."

"This mofo is serious about this, huh?" Ciara mumbled to herself. Then she shouted back, "Shawn, don't you think we need to talk about this a little more?"

After walking out of the bedroom, she slowly descended the stairs while gripping the banister, hoping she didn't faint from the realization of Shawn leaving her.

"You're not going to change the way I feel. This is something I have to get out of my system."

"Out of your system! I'm your wife, Shawn, and this isn't like a hangover from drinking or a game that you can't beat on that damn Playstation. This is real life shit! How can you run away when things get tough between us? We're supposed to get through this together as husband and wife. We haven't exhausted all of our options yet." Ciara paused to take a deep breath. "I'm so sorry. I'm just upset about everything."

Ciara tried to hug him, but he pushed her arms from around his shoulders. Shawn had his mind made up, and not even the tears from his wife could stop him. The coldness had already started to settle in his heart.

"Yeah, well, I'll give you plenty of time to think about it," Shawn replied, before heading towards the door.

"After all we've been through?" Ciara's emotions were taking over again. "After all the times I've forgiven you for cheating on me? After the abortions we paid for because you were out cheating with everybody and their momma?"

Shawn stood there impassive. "I'll talk to you later. Good

luck with everything."

And with that, Shawn exited the house and closed the door behind him, giving less than two shits about what Ciara was talking about.

Immediately, Ciara rushed to her phone so she could call Kim again.

"Okay, two can play this game, and I'm not going to lose, motherfucker!"

She quickly dialed Kim's number.

"Damn, am I the only number you know? Did you forget about 9-1-1? And you know you hung up on me, right?"

"Never mind that. We're going out tonight, Kim."

"What? Miss Goodie Two Shoes is going to step foot inside a Chicago club tonight?"

"Shawn is about to see how the old Ciara operates. Who the hell does he think he's playing with?"

"The old Ciara would've set his clothes on fire and fucked his brother," Kim added.

"No, that's what the old and new Kim would've done."

"You're right about that shit! Ms. Kim keeps it on and popping."

"I'll come and get you at about twelve. Make sure you're ready," Ciara said, ignoring Kim's comment and hanging up on her once again.

******

It was about 12:30 a.m. when Ciara and Kim arrived at Club Ontourage.

"Damn, I'm in sexy man heaven right now. I haven't

seen a brother that was ugly or even okay looking yet."

"Me either. The stars are definitely out tonight. Let's get a drink."

As Ciara and Kim made their way to the bar, pants were bulging and heads were turning as every man stood in awe looking at the two beautiful women. Kim had on a peanut butter colored strapless Prada dress with matching peanut butter Prada boots that came all the way up to her succulent thighs. Although Kim's dress was fitting that ass like an O.J. Simpson glove, the matching Prada purse she swung loosely on her arm was what had the haters on ten.

Ciara was on another level with her fit. She had on a red Jay Godfrey dress that tied up around the neck, exposing her back, with red and white Chanel boots that matched her red and white Chanel purse. The onlookers knew she'd had the dress custom made because it fit well to her body. With the dress stopping right beneath her booty, all Ciara had to do was bend over and she would be leaving with a millionaire tonight.

The music was loud and the club was jumping as the crowd repeated the lyrics to Biggie's classic remix "One More Chance".

"What are you ladies going to have tonight?" the bartender with dreadlocks asked Kim.

"I'll have a Long Island Ice Tea."

"And for you, miss?"

"Water, please," Ciara replied.

"Water? No, she'll have the same thing I'm having, and add a Blue Motherfucker, as well! Loosen up, Ciara. Damn! You're making me feel tight, and it's bad enough already that I have this tight-ass dress on. I thought you were trying to party tonight? Don't be in here acting like Ms. I Only Fucks with Seven-figure Niggas!"

As Ciara and Kim laughed, enjoyed the music, and sipped on their chilled drinks, an uncomfortable-looking man approached them.

"Excuse me, ladies, but my eyes have seen the glory, and I just have to dance with one of you," he said, then stood there waiting on a response.

Ciara and Kim looked at each other and then back at the man before replying in unison, "No, thank you."

"Fuck you two stuck-up chicks. I like white girls anyway."

"Whatever, dude, the L4L area is over there!"

The man didn't respond as Kim pointed to a corner where a couple of square looking men were sitting. Instead, he walked off.

"Girl, you're crazy! What the hell is L4L?" Ciara asked.

"Lames 4 Life."

Ciara almost fell on the floor laughing.

"And I don't know who he thought he was going to get, wearing that old-ass shirt and them tight-ass nut hugger pants."

"Tell me about it, girl," Ciara cosigned.

"Oh my goodness! Look at him, Ciara."

Ciara's face froze as she looked at the man Kim was pointing out to her. He stood about 6'3", weighed about 225 pounds, was dark skinned, and had an athletic build, a low haircut, brown eyes, a goatee, and a smile that could brighten up a funeral on Sunday morning Christmas day.

"I bet he has a big…"

"Damn, Kim, slow down! Do you need another drink? You've only seen the man for five seconds and already you're talking about what he's working with in his pants."

"I already know he has to be working with something," Kim seductively bit her bottom lip, amazed by the gentleman's appearance.

The two women chuckled like two schoolgirls as they watched the attractive man walk across the club.

"Yeah, you're probably right, Kim. He has to be working with a monster."

"I don't get good-looking brothers like that anymore," Kim complained. "I think I'm falling off, girl. I only attract lowlifes."

"Oh, that's not your type anymore?" Ciara joked.

"I'm serious."

"I know," Ciara replied. "Well, if it's like that, go and talk to him."

"Hell no! As good as I look, he better bring his fine ass over here. I always had to chase the cute ones. He will have to notice me this time."

"Well, I think you're about to get your wish, because he's walking this way."

"What?" Kim said, fumbling with the red straw in her drink.

"Hello, ladies. How are you doing tonight?"

"We're good," Ciara replied, then turned her head away from the man.

"I was wondering if…"

Before he could finish his sentence, Kim interrupted him.

"Yes, I'd love to dance."

This fast-ass hoe, Ciara thought, while trying to hold her fake Hollywood smile. *I thought her hot ass was going to get chased tonight.*

As Kim and the handsome gentleman danced, Ciara watched their every move. *That's one fine brother, but I shouldn't be looking at him like that because I have a man. I bet Shawn is just playing with me and will be over this immature phase soon. I love him, but I can't wait on him forever.*

Ciara's eyes couldn't leave Kim and the attractive gentleman. The smell of his Sean John cologne still lingered around the table. Kim, on the other hand, was thinking about what she wanted to do to him later.

"You're a great dancer," Kim mentioned, observing the gentleman's moves.

"Thank you. You're not so bad yourself…Miss?"

"I'm so rude. I didn't even give you my name. It's Kim… Kim Morris."

"Kim Morris, pleased to meet you. My name is Decorey Swift."

Pleased to meet your sexy ass, too, Kim thought, but responded by saying, "It's a pleasure to meet you, as well," while looking into his eyes.

"Would you care for another drink, Kim?"

"Sure, I'd like that."

Taking Kim by the hand, Decorey led her back to the table where Ciara sat impatiently waiting.

"Ciara, Decorey and I are going to get something to drink. Did you want something?"

"Sure, get me a Hurricane, no ice." As she watched them walk away, she softly mumbled to herself, "I guess they got well acquainted during their little dance."

"So tell me a little about yourself, Kim."

"Well, I was born and raised here in Illinois. No children, no job, and I'm very single."

He was quiet because the "very single" line threw him off.

"Interesting," Decorey hesitantly replied.

"How about yourself, Decorey?"

"I own Swift & Swift Construction Company out in Bolingbrook, and I'm originally from the Southside of Chicago."

"Southside, huh? I really don't mess with any southsiders. Y'all are too crazy for me out there," she replied, while thinking, *He's good looking and getting paid. Upgrade me, daddy.*

"What the hell is taking them so long? Did they have to get the drinks from Mississippi?" Ciara said, finishing up her Long Island.

Just then, her cell phone began to vibrate in her purse. When she looked at the display, she saw it was Shawn calling. She knew he would call sooner or later, but she didn't think it would be that soon.

"What do you want, Shawn?" Although smiling from ear to ear, she tried to act irritated about his call.

"I just wanted to tell you that I'm finished moving all of my things out of the house. If you need to get in contact with me, just call my cell phone."

Click!

"Ain't this about a bitch?" Ciara was about to snap, but Kim and Decorey interrupted her.

"Hey, who was that?" Kim inquired, while handing the drink to her.

"Nobody important."

Decorey reached out his hand towards Ciara. "I don't think we were introduced. My name is Decorey Swift, and yours?"

"My name is Ciara," she responded with a feisty attitude.

"Do you have a last name, Ciara?"

"Are you the police or something, Decorey? Why do

you need to know my last name?"

"Relax, Ciara! What's wrong? Was that who I think it was on the phone, because you're tripping?" Kim inquired.

Ciara didn't respond. Instead, she stared off in a daze.

"Well, I'm sorry, Ciara. I didn't mean to offend you."

She had played it off. She didn't want Kim or Decorey in her business.

"No, no, don't apologize, Decorey, because I was totally rude. My last name is Blackwell."

"And she is happily married," Kim added.

Decorey paused for a second. He knew that name rang a bell.

Kim is on one tonight, Ciara thought. "Yes, I'm married, Decorey, and thank you, Channel Six."

For the rest of the night, Kim tried to impress Decorey, but her efforts went unnoticed because his focus was strictly on Ciara. He started to watch Ciara's every move. Throughout the night, Ciara noticed Decorey's stares, but she really didn't pay too much attention to it because she was still pissed off about Shawn's call.

"It's getting late and I need to get up early for work. I think I'm going to call it a night, ladies."

"You're the boss, and nothing starts until you make it in anyway, Decorey."

"Yeah, but it's late, and I need to be heading home."

Kim looked over at Ciara and then back at him. "Decorey, if you don't mind, could you please give me a ride home?"

Ciara's eyes became big, as if she'd seen a ghost. Then she began to choke while finishing up her drink. *Kim is at it already*.

"Sure, but didn't you come here with Ciara?"

"No, I was here with someone else, but she left early."

"It's not a problem. I'll take you home."

"Well, boo boo, I don't mean any harm, but I think Decorey lives closer to me. Besides, I don't want you to get home late because Shawn might get worried."

Decorey looked at Ciara mysteriously when he heard the mention of Shawn's name.

I know she didn't, Ciara thought. *I should kick her right in the back of her hating-ass head.*

"Nice meeting you, Ciara. We had a great time."

"Same here, Decorey. Drive safe."

As the two began to walk away, Kim turned around and gave Ciara an "I'll call you" gesture with her left hand.

******

Ciara did about 85 MPH all the way home.

What a night! First, Shawn calls and tells me that he's completely moved out, and then Kim hates on me at the club. I should go and break all of her windows out, smoke a blunt, and go sleep this bullshit off. No, I'm tripping. I have a man, and he's a good man at that. He just doesn't know what he wants right now. I have to just wait and see what's going to happen with us, Ciara thought as she scanned through the radio stations, stopping when she came across "If You Think You're Lonely Now" by Bobby Womack.

What the hell? Oh, this is definitely a bad night.

Ciara turned the radio down, grabbed a pre-rolled blunt that she had ready for Kim and herself after they left the club, and smoked the rest of the way home.

******

The next morning, she woke up to the sound of her doorbell repeatedly ringing.

"Who the hell is it?"

She was still trying to wake up as she went to answer the door. A well-dressed woman stood at the front door, while Ciara looked through the foggy peephole.

Is that Shawn's car? Hold on, I know this isn't his stripper hoe. Ciara swung the door open. "Yes, can I help you?"

"Hey, I know you don't know me, but Shawn sent me over here to get his mail, Ciara."

"Who the hell are you?" The popping sound of the woman's gum made Ciara want to snatch her by her head. "And how do you know my name?"

"I'm Pink," the female said proudly.

"Pink? Pink what?"

"That's my name. What do you have to say about it?" Pink asked, looking Ciara up and down.

"What kind of name is that?"

"I got a pretty pink pussy. That's where I got the name from! Plies made that song about me, girl."

Ciara knew she was totally caught off of her square by Pink. *What in the hell? I'm looking like a crackhead gone wild, while Shawn's bitch is at the door fresh from head to toe.*

Pink had on a brand-new Juicy outfit with matching sunglasses. She was about 5'5", 140 pounds, brown skinned, with long jet-black hair, and a tattoo on her right arm that said M.O.N. (money over niggas).

She looks like she came straight from Jay-Z's video, and I look like a damn runaway slave. This is so bogus, Ciara thought.

"Shawn doesn't have any mail over here, Pinky."

"Yes, he does, and the name is Pink. He left it on the counter last night when we were grabbing the rest of his stuff."

"So he let you in my house last night?"

"Yeah, why not?"

"Why not? Bitch, don't you ever come in here and…"

Ciara wasn't able to complete her sentence before Pink put her hand up. "First of all, don't get mad at me. And second, you need to calm down because it's too early in the morning to be hearing all of that. Goodness, I'll just tell Shawn to come and get his own mail," Pink replied, as she walked away.

Ciara stood there in shock, while watching as Pink descended the porch steps and got back into Shawn's car. The sight of Pink's hips switching from side to side annoyed her. All of a sudden, she came to her senses and ran at full speed out of the house. In the process, she managed to grab a stone that was lying by a nearby bush. Noticing Ciara's actions, Pink quickly pulled off. Ciara threw the stone at the car, but it didn't have the distance to hit it. Enraged, Ciara raced back into the house and slammed the door.

"That bitch! That ugly bitch! I can't believe this! Fuck! No, I'm about to go and kick that bitch's ass."

Ciara ran into her bedroom and called her best friend. The answering machine picked up on the first ring.

"Hi, this is Kim. Leave a message."

Beep!

"Wake up, Kim! I'm about to go kill Shawn's little slut girlfriend. Pick up the phone!"

Kim picked up as Ciara continued yelling over the answering machine.

"What are you yelling about, Ciara?" Kim asked in a panic.

"Get up! Get up right now, Kim!"

"What's the matter?"

"Shawn's stripper hoe just came over here!"

"What? Are you serious?"

"Yes, and she was in his car, too."

"Did you whoop that trick, Ciara?"

"No, I let her get away!"

"What? You let her get away? Why didn't you drag that bitch to the lake?"

"She caught me off guard. I'm on my way to get you, Kim!"

Kim knew Ciara should've taken care of Pink right then and there, but she knew Ciara was more hurt than angry. *My girl is gonna have a nervous breakdown because of Shawn's cheating ass,* Kim thought.

******

"Ciara, we've been driving around for over an hour, and we haven't made it to Shawn's house yet? Wait a minute. Do you even know where he lives?"

Ciara looked over at Kim and smiled.

"Ciara! You got me out here looking like this, thinking we about to bust some heads, and you don't even know where Shawn lives?"

The two of them burst into laughter.

"Girl, you're a nut. Talk to me, C. What's the deal? Are you gonna be okay?"

She knew firsthand that Ciara allowed her feelings to get in the way of her well-being. At this moment, she wasn't quite sure if her girl would go crazy trying to get Shawn to come back home.

"I can't believe it's really over between us."

"Maybe it's just something that Shawn is going through right now and it'll pass."

"Yeah, but it's different this time because he had another woman in our home. The home we once lived in together. I just wish he--" Ciara's words began to break up as tears rolled down her cheeks. "I just wish he would've given me some closure."

"I know, but you have to be stronger than that. Keep your head up, and when he realizes that he messed up, he'll be back begging on his knees."

Kim knew her friend wouldn't get over Shawn anytime soon, and she wanted to be as supportive as possible during her friend's troubled time.

Chapter 3

"So when is it your turn, Patrice?"

"You know I hate it when you call me by my real name, Shawn."

"I'm sorry, but right now, I'm being so serious. I promised you that I would leave everything behind for you. When will you do the same for me?"

"I told you that I'm going to stop stripping in a couple of months."

"I'm not talking about that. I'm talking about your husband. I thought I was the most important person in your life?"

"You are. You and Ben Franklin."

"I'm serious, Pink."

"I know, baby, but it can't happen overnight. Just give me a little more time, and I promise we'll be together with no interferences."

Just at that moment, Pink's cell phone began to ring, interrupting their conversation.

"See what I mean? He's not over you. He needs you. And I'm starting to think you're not over him either."

"How can you say that, baby? You're the only person that matters to me."

"I hope so," Shawn replied, as he lay back in the bed.

"Wake me up before you leave out."

******

"All I need is fifty-two cents on pump three. Can a brother get some gas for his car?"

"Get the hell out of our face, Toby. You stink! Where's your car anyway, and since when do you have one?"

"I parked it down the street, Ciara."

"Down the street? Do we look crazy to you? You've been walking since we graduated high school. You must think we're crazy."

"Are you ready, Ciara, because he's getting on my last nerve?"

"You act like you're better than me or something, Kim, because you have on clean clothes and have about twenty dollars in your pocket."

"All I'm saying is that you can't mix shit and Curve cologne together and think you smell like roses, Toby."

"Leave him alone! Here, Toby. Now go and mind your business," Ciara said, as she handed him two dollars.

"You just helped a brother out, Ciara. I promise I'm gonna pay you back."

"Don't worry about it."

"You just helped me out, so I have to pay you back. You act like it's hard for me to hustle up nine quarters."

"Nine quarters?" Kim repeated. "Take your dusty ass on, Toby!"

"You wish you had a man like me on your team. Don't you, Kim?"

"Fool, please! You need to try and get on team Burger King or team Wendy's with your broke ass."

"One day I'm gonna have it all, Kim. Watch me! I'm

gonna get my shit together, and when I do, I'm gonna laugh at your ass while you're at the bus stop fucking for rides."

"Toby, you got me real fucked up! I'm not one of these crackheads out here you be fucking with. I'll give your ass a buck fifty!"

"Well, give it here, because I'm trying to stack my money up!"

"You're broke and dumb, Toby. A buck fifty is when you slice someone in the face with a razor. My cousin from New York told me about it, bum!"

Toby laughed. "Ha! You don't know anybody from New York. I haven't seen you in none of P-Diddy's videos before. Whatever you say, Kim. A buck fifty. I'm outta here. And thank you again, CIARA!"

"Whatever, idiot."

"Why do you always give Toby money when you see him?"

"I think it's embarrassing that he's out here begging for money like that."

"I think he's a crackhead and always will be one, if you ask me. He hasn't been the same since they jumped on him in high school."

"I remember that. He stole Big Chris's car, and they tried to beat him into a coma that day. But that isn't funny, Kim."

"I know it isn't," Kim replied, with her hands in the air and fingers crossed. "Hey, I'm going out tonight."

"Again? This is your third time this week."

"Last time I checked I was a G.A.W."

"What's a G.A.W.?"

"A grown-ass woman."

"I'm not trying to be your mother. I just think you kick

it too much."

"Too much for who?"

"Forget I even said anything."

"I'm just playing. You've been so sensitive lately. What's the matter?"

"I just haven't been myself. I feel lonely and I miss Shawn so much," Ciara replied.

"Here we go again. I know you do, but I think it's time for you to move on without him."

"Move on!"

"Yeah, did-did I stutter? All I'm saying is that Shawn is out doing his thing."

"What do you mean, doing his thing?"

"He's holding up his side of the open-door relationship. Remember, Ciara? I don't want you to go out there and open your legs for just anybody, but I think it's time you find a friend for yourself. You got half of the city trying to get with you, girl."

"I know, but I don't have time for bullshit right now. I need someone that understands me."

"No, what you need is a friend with benefits! I know that little lady of yours is screaming for some attention," Kim said, while glancing down at Ciara's crotch.

"She's not screaming yet, but she's down there talking shit. I think you're right, Kim. It's about time I find someone to put on my team," Ciara replied, feeling more confident.

"I think I might know the right person for you."

"I don't know about that. Just don't find me someone that's fresh out of prison," Ciara responded, then took a sip of her Aquafina."

"You might need a thug in your life, but people that are the same don't usually get alone."

"What? You think I'm a thug or something like that?"

"Now, I'm not the one to gossip, but you're the only girl I knew in the seventh grade that could shoot a gun and deactivate a car alarm. So, you might be a little too much for a thug come to think of it."

"Whatever! Just make sure he has all of his teeth and a job this time."

"Don't even worry about it, Ciara. You know I got everything handled on my end."

******

"Why do you have to come home so late?"

Shawn was still on his duty of badgering Pink about her sketchy behavior.

"It's a part of my job, baby. I have to work long hours at night so I can get more money."

"That's just an excuse."

"An excuse? So you think I shouldn't make any money? Or better yet, do you want me to stop stripping all together?"

Shawn took a deep breath as he sat down on the edge of the bed. "All I'm saying is I would like to spend more time with you."

"I know you do, Shawn, but it wasn't a problem before. Why did things suddenly change with us?"

"I don't know. I guess my feelings are different for you now."

"I don't know if that's good or bad."

"It's good, Pink, but I just hate it when other men have the opportunity to look at what I have."

"Is someone a little jealous?"

"No, but this has to come to an end," Shawn replied, as

he stood up.

"Well, I think we're going to have a problem, because this is the way I put food on my table," she shot back.

"*Our* table. Remember, it's *our* table now. You're not in this by yourself, and I'm not going to let you go without."

"But, I've never been the type to depend on anyone, and you know that, baby. It's been that way since I was fourteen. I've been hustling and surviving in these streets before I met you. Can't just change my ways overnight for anyone. This is how I get down. Love me or leave me, Shawn. It's your call."

"So let me get a good understanding of this. You're basically saying you're not going to stop stripping?"

"Basically."

Shawn stood there speechless for a few moments. He was beginning to have second thoughts about moving out of his home to be with Pink. Apparently, she was not ready for what he wanted.

"Forget this," he finally said, then grabbed his car keys and stormed out of the door.

"Oh well, he'll get over it," Pink mumbled, as she grabbed a half-full bottle of Grey Goose and poured the strong drink slowly into her glass.

Chapter 4

"You know I'm done messing with you, Kim. Stop laughing, because it isn't funny. Why did you introduce him to me?"

"Okay, wait. I'm going to stop laughing and explain."

"Explain. Please explain!"

"I thought he wasn't that bad, Ciara, and I thought you just wanted to get out of the house and get some air."

"Get some air! Everywhere I went, he went. I was trying to be nice, but he was annoying as hell. He was bright and terrible. Kim, you know I don't like light-skinned men. He looked like a big-ass banana next to me. He had on some Air Force Two's, and I didn't even know they made those. On top of all that, his ass didn't have any money!"

"I know, because he asked me for a couple of dollars until next weekend."

"You should've just hooked me up with crackhead Toby."

"I know, girl, but next time, I'm going to do you right."

"I would've never done you like that. I'll get over it, but I have to get some sleep first. I'm about to take a bath and lie down for a second, so call me back."

"I'll call you when I get back from the doctor's office in the morning."

"What's wrong with you? I hope you're not pregnant

                                    Discombobulated
with Eric's ugly-ass baby."

"Ugly! It's impossible for a man that sexy to produce an ugly seed."

"Well, why are you going to the free clinic?"

"I'm not going to the free clinic. I'm just getting a normal check-up by my doctor, that's all."

"Whatever. Just call me when you make it home."

Ciara placed her phone on the charger and headed towards the bathroom so she could rejuvenate and forget about her terrible date. She made a mental note never to trust Kim to set her up on a blind date. She was about to run some bath water, when her phone rang. It was Shawn.

"After your little stripper hoe used and abused you, then you call me," Ciara spat into the phone. She decided against saying a friendly hello and went straight into attitude mode.

"No, it's not like that, baby. I just really need to see you."

"Fuck you, Shawn. I'm having company tonight."

"Yeah right, and Tupac is alive, too. I saw him at the car wash earlier." Shawn let out a deep laugh, as if Ciara wasn't even on the other end.

"You know what? Goodbye, Shawn!"

Ciara closed her cell phone, ending their conversation, and that made her feel good. She was going to take control over this relationship and make him work hard for the good thing he left behind.

"Next," Shawn said, as he began to dial another number. *Pick up the phone*, he thought, while shuffling through his CD collection in the car.

"Hello," the sad voice on the other end answered.

"Can I come by and see you tonight, sexy? I miss you."

The voice on the other end was silent for a few seconds before responding, "I guess you can come over, Shawn."

"Okay, I'll be there in five minutes."

Shawn's heart was racing as he drove down the dark, one-way street. He almost hit a stray cat while dialing on his phone as he pulled up to the house.

Shawn wanted to make this quick. He wasn't trying to be out there all night just to bust a nut. Shawn silently planned, while placing an Altoid mint in his mouth.

"Come on, baby. I'm outside."

A short, slender person quickly opened the front door and waved for Shawn to come inside.

"Come on! I want to go for a ride!" Shawn yelled through his passenger window.

"Okay, I'll be right out."

Shawn quickly sprayed some air freshener throughout his car as he waited for his company to arrive. The person carefully got into the car, trying not to drag their coat into the puddle of water. Once the door closed, Shawn sped off.

"So what did you want to see me about?"

"I miss you, baby. Is that a problem or something?"

"Fool, please, you've been singing that same tune for the last six years. You've been playing with my emotions for too long. I don't think I'm ready to go through this with you again. I had you all to myself once before, and then you had a change of heart. No, I refuse to put myself through it again."

"I know I've hurt you, but things have changed with me."

"How have they changed? I haven't been number one, two, or three. I've just been some convenient ass for you. I've been some 'Oh, I want something different tonight' ass, huh? You can't have your cake and eat it, too. At least not with me."

"Calm the fuck down. You're not even giving me a chance to express myself."

"Okay, proceed."

"I love you, and I always have. You mean a lot to me. You know that, and I know that. Why must we go through this every time you feel that I'm not focused on you?"

"I'm just tired of this open-door policy with you. How many doors can you have opened at once?" There were several moments of silence. "No comment? That's just what I thought. I'm leaving. Goodnight!"

"Wait a minute. I'm done playing games out here. You just have to believe me. I want to share everything with you. You've been there for me when I wasn't there for myself. I owe you that much credit."

"But what about, Ciara?"

"Ciara is a different story, baby. I've grown to love Ciara, but I've always loved you."

Shawn waited patiently for a response. The only sound that could be heard was J. Holiday playing in the background as they sat in the car watching the windows fog up.

"I just don't understand you. Why can't you see that I want to be with you? I miss you. I miss us."

"I'm sorry about the way I've been treating you," Shawn said, as he reached his arms out for a hug. "Damn, you smell so good."

Shawn couldn't resist the sexual tension that was building. He put his head back and unzipped his pants. There was no need for him to ask or beg his companion to give him a blowjob. The unzipping of his pants was all that needed to be done. His companion got right on the task. The rapid and intense head movement had him weak and at a disadvantage. Just the slurping sound alone was enough for Shawn to explode.

"Go down further on it, baby. Yeah, just like that. Keep going. Please don't stop."

Shawn was too deep into the pleasure being bestowed upon him to notice someone walking up to the car. It was Toby coming over to bum some money, or whatever he could get, but when he knocked on the window, Toby witnessed more than he wanted.

Shawn was in shock when he opened his eyes and noticed who was at the window.

"What the fuck!" Toby said, looking intently at the person's head that rose up from Shawn's lap. Toby was speechless.

"Get the fuck out of here!" Shawn screamed. It only took him a split second to start the car and screech off.

"I can't believe this one! No, I have to stop taking these drugs because I think my mind is playing tricks on me. Like my brother from another mother, Marvin Gaye, once said, 'What's going on?'"

Toby grabbed the half pint of gin out of his back pocket and finished the bottle in one gulp.

"What's wrong, Shawn?"

"What's wrong? Are you serious, Byron? He just saw us!"

"So what, he's just a damn fiend. Let me finish my duty, boo."

Shawn's dick went limp just at the sight of Toby seeing him with another man. As much as he wanted Byron to finish him off, he had to make him stop. It didn't matter how good the head was, because there was no way Shawn could have gotten another hard-on after being exposed.

"Not right now, Byron. I'm taking you back home."

"Home? See, you're fucking ashamed of me!" Byron copped an attitude and folded his arms across his chest.

There was complete silence in the car on the way back to Byron's house. Shawn always kept things in order, but he didn't want this secret to leak out.

I have to get rid of Toby. He's going to ruin my life, Shawn thought, while reaching underneath his seat and pulling out a black .380.

"Oh my God, Shawn! What's that for?"

"Don't worry about it. Everything is going to be okay."

"So why do you have that gun?" Byron couldn't understand why Shawn was so upset.

"It's nothing, Byron. Nothing at all."

Byron and Shawn had been messing around for about six years. Byron considered himself the cream of the crop. He stood about 5'7" and weighed 110 pounds. If the wind blew too hard, it was over for his light ass. He was brown skinned with long black hair that he kept in a ponytail. He only wore designer outfits, and sped up and down the Chicago streets in his burnt orange Pontiac G6 that had Winnie the Pooh stuffed bears in the back window. He was a true man diva indeed.

******

The next day, Toby just had to tell somebody about his crazy experience last night.

"Bet me if you think I'm lying, Chris!"

"Toby, I told you to stop smoking that shit so much, especially when I'm not there to smoke it with you."

"You think I'm lying, don't you? Shawn Blackwell was in the car with another man last night, getting his knob polished."

"Whatever, and if he was, so what? That's his business, not yours. If he's gay, oh well."

"Oh well? Don't you know I run these streets? Nothing happens around here until I say so. I'm like the Chicago version of Bumpy Johnson. I got the cops on my team and all of the storeowners love me. I got to keep things under control out here."

"No, you run in these streets, Toby. You don't run them. We're crackheads. Who in the hell is gonna listen to us anyway?"

"Okay, you think I'm playing? I'll blow everything up around here."

Toby lifted up his shirt, exposing a pint of liquor he had in his front pocket.

"Not before we try to smoke everything first," Chris said with a smirk on his face.

"You got that right," Toby replied, giving Chris dap. "Let's go. I think school is about to let out, and I know those kids got some money left from lunch or something."

They both began to walk towards the elementary school, when Toby spotted Shawn's car.

"Hey, Chris!"

"What? What's wrong?"

"Don't look now, but I think that's Shawn's car over there."

"Where?" Chris questioned, looking around.

"I told you don't look, fool!"

When Shawn realized Toby had spotted him, he burned rubber pulling out of the parking lot.

"Forget this. I'm not going to the school. I have to lay low for a minute."

"Lay low? Man, Shawn isn't worried about you! Forget it. Since you think Shawn and the CIA is after you, I'm gone. I'll catch your story on *Cops* later on."

"Hold on!"

"What now? I'm not going with you because you're making me nervous. I have to go and get me some money!"

"I wasn't going to ask you to go with me."

"Well, what is it? I have places to go and things to smoke."

"Do you have a couple of dollars I can borrow until later on?"

"You can take a monkey out of the zoo, but you can't take the zoo out of the monkey," Chris replied, as he walked away, while shaking his head in disbelief.

Chapter 5

"What do you want me to do, Byron? I'm trying my best to make this work. I thought you of all people would understand my situation."

"What do I want you to do? I want you to make your mind up. I need to know if you're with me or against me."

"I don't know what to do. I'm in a tough spot with all of this bullshit!" Shawn's anger began to grow as he thought more about his confounded situation.

"How are you in a tough spot? I'm the one hiding and ducking around corners late at night to be with you. I'm not the one who's ashamed of what I am. I'm a fucking homosexual! I'm nothing more or nothing less."

As Byron stood up from the couch, Shawn grabbed his arm. "Wait, I'm not ashamed of us. I just have a lot of things going on in my life right now."

"So why can't we see each other during the day? Why do we have to get hotel rooms out of town or late at night? You need to wake up and smell the damn coffee."

Before he knew it, he backhanded Byron to the floor. Still in shock from the blow, Byron scooted his frail body a safe distance away from Shawn's reach and stared back at him from his position on the floor.

Steven Morgan

"I'm sorry. I don't know what's wrong with me." After realizing what had happened, he kneeled down to comfort his boy toy.

"Get the hell out of my house! Get out now!"

Seeing his handprint on the side of Byron's face, Shawn could only respect his demand as he got up and left. A million things were running through Shawn's mind. He could have stayed and pleaded with him more, but Shawn was tired of apologizing for his actions when he had no clue as to why or what he was doing.

He was caught up in a confused state of mind. There was a war going on inside of him, and he didn't know which side would come out the victor. His main battle was between his love for women and his lust for men. When he needed someone to talk with the most, he found himself alone and afraid to admit his lifestyle. The only thing he was certain of was that he had to make some changes soon, before he witnessed his life crumbling down before his eyes.

Shawn began scrolling through his cell phone as he walked to his car. The only person he could think of calling was Ciara, so he slowly dialed her number. Only two rings went through before she answered.

"I'm busy, Shawn. What the fuck do you want?"

"Nothing, I just wanted to hear your voice. Is that a problem?"

"Well, you heard it, right? So, goodbye!"

"Wait a minute, Ciara! I just wanted to know if you would like to go out to dinner and talk."

Ciara couldn't believe what she was hearing, as she pulled the phone away from her ear and looked at the receiver.

"Shawn, what do you hang your clothes on, baby?"

"Hangers, why?"

Click!

"This bitch hung up on me!" he said out loud, but to no one in particular. "Forget it. I didn't want to be bothered with her ass anyway."

Shawn became more enraged when he tried to call Pink and her voicemail came on with R. Kelly's "Leave Your Name" playing in the background.

"This is Pink. Leave a message."

Beep!

"Hey, lady, call me back when you get this message. I miss you. Bye."

An incoming call beeped in as he was finishing up his message to Pink. He clicked over, answering with an agitated voice.

"Hello!"

"I'm sorry about hanging up on you. Do you really want to go out and talk?" Ciara asked in a low, seductive voice.

"Yes, because I really want to make this marriage work. I know I haven't been fair in this relationship. I've been selfish and immature about everything. I'm sorry, baby."

Ciara was so excited that she didn't know how to respond. She loved being able to say that she was married and was not going to allow anyone to destroy her life. At the same time, Shawn was just happy someone answered his call because he didn't feel like being alone or having to jack off. Both had their own motives that would one day collide and explode.

"I'll be ready around eight o'clock. Is that time good for you?"

"Perfect. I'll be there at eight," Shawn replied.

"Bye, baby."

I knew he would be back. He couldn't stay away from me. He knows where home is, and besides, I got that good-

good, Ciara thought, as she stood in the mirror admiring her physique.

Her night began with two chilled glasses of Moet, rose petals in a hot, steamy bath, and soft music by Luther Vandross. The mood was right, and Ciara was ready to get her man back. But, before she could prepare for the night, she had to run out and get a pair of pantyhose to go with her dress.

After stopping her bath water, she left out the door to head to the store. While walking to her car, she spotted the neighbor's pit bull, Smoke, and noticed he was off of his chain.

She mumbled a prayer. "God, please don't let this dog bite me!" She looked around to see if she could grab a stick or something before Smoke made it to her. "Get out of here, Smoke! Move! Bernie, come and get your damn dog!"

Now, Bernie had to be about one hundred and sixty-six years old. He was sweet, old, and perverted. There had been plenty of times when Shawn felt Bernie said some inappropriate things to Ciara about her body. The shabby-looking man walked out of the front door of his house yelling at his dog, who sniffed Ciara's shoes right before lifting his hind leg as if he was about to pee on her.

"Not on my new Air Max, Smoke!"

"Smoke, get your ass away from her! I said, get!"

Smoke put his leg down and ran to where Bernie was on the front porch.

"I'm sorry about that, Ciara. I'm not going to let Smoke do anything to your gorgeous body."

Ignoring Bernie, she quickly got into her car. Her nerves were on edge as she drove to the store and her stomach was doing flips. She felt as anxious as she did when she and Shawn had their first date many years ago.

After listening to a couple of songs from Mary J Blige's

My Life CD, she finally made it to her destination. She stormed right in and bumped into a man walking ahead of her.

"Excuse me!"

"I'm so sorry, sir, but don't I know you? Derrick is your name, right?" Ciara asked.

"No, it's Decorey."

Ciara noticed that Decorey was still on point, just like the last time she saw him in the club. He was looking extremely handsome this night, but Ciara had Shawn waiting on her. No time for small talk.

"Well, I don't mean to be rude, Decorey, but I'm kind of in a rush. I have somewhere to be in about an hour."

"Can I at least exchange numbers with you?"

At that point, Decorey wasn't taking "no" for an answer, as he handed Ciara his business card.

"Here's my card. You can reach me at any of those numbers on there."

"Okay, here's my number, too, but I really have to get going."

"No problem. I'll give you a call sometime this weekend, if that's okay?"

Ciara rushed out of the door without buying her pantyhose or even giving him a reply.

Damn, what's her problem? Decorey thought.

Meanwhile, Ciara stood outside frantically searching through her purse. She was looking for a cigar to roll her blunt, but all she thumbed through was an old pack of gum, her wallet, keys, pepper spray, and lip gloss. Everything but what she wanted. Her mind traveled back to the handsome and mysterious Decorey. As fine as he was with his smooth skin, she knew she should not have given him her number. First, he danced all up on Kim at the club and then took her home.

Steven Morgan

Anything could have happened that night. Most importantly, she didn't need another man because Shawn had come to his senses and wanted her back. Or so she thought.

Unsuccessful at finding a cigar, she backtracked into the store. She knew Shawn wanted her to stop smoking, but she needed something to soothe her jitters.

When Ciara walked into the store to purchase a Swisher, the clerk watched her carefully as her hips swung from side to side.

"How do you do tonight, madam?"

"I'm cool, Abdul. How are you?"

"You know, in my country, pretty women like you would be considered royalty."

"Oh that's so sweet, but why would I be considered royalty?"

"Because of your perfect, round bottom."

"What kind of shit is that to say, Abdul? I should come back there and snatch your Arab ass from behind that glass!"

"No, miss, I didn't mean to offend you," he replied, while raising his hands in a gesture to show that he meant no harm.

"What the hell do I look like? I'm not one of these trifling-ass bust downs that be walking in here! I'm going to catch your ass when you're not behind that glass, Abdul!"

As Ciara turned to leave the store, the girl who had been standing behind her yelled, "Who are you talking about? I'm not a bust down!"

"Mind your motherfucking business. I wasn't even talking to you, chick!" Ciara replied, while mean-mugging her. "But, if you feel like I'm talking about you, so be it."

At that point, Ciara was ready for war.

"Ciara, you might scare all of these other bitches around

here, but I'll tap that ass!" another girl yelled, as she stood with a small group.

"Well, get to tapping then, Faye, because I've been waiting to get in your ass for a good minute now. You and your dick-sucking friend Peaches stole my leather coat from Ronnie's birthday party two years ago."

"Bitch, I don't have to steal shit. I got money!"

Ciara walked toward the group of women. "Enough with all this talking. Let's go outside, Faye."

Ciara then headed towards the door, waiting on Faye to follow her outside. Faye glanced over at her friends, but no one said a word. Faye, who knew about Ciara's reputation in the neighborhood, quickly had a change of heart.

"I don't have time for this shit. Go on about your business, Ciara."

"Yeah, that's what I thought, chick. I should snatch one of them kitchen braids out of your damn head!"

"Please, just leave, miss!"

"Fuck you, Abdul, and fuck who sent you, too!"

You could hear the door handle hit the brick wall as Ciara stormed outside.

Ciara got in her car and drove back home. For a second time, she forgot to purchase her pantyhose. Shawn would just have easy access tonight. As she made it through her front door, her phone began to vibrate. She looked at it to see Kim's name flashing on the screen.

"Hey, what's up, girl?"

"Nothing," Kim responded in a soft tone.

"You don't sound like your normal self. Talk to me. I know something's bothering you."

"I just have a lot of things on my mind, and I need someone to talk to."

"I hope you're not pregnant."

"No, I'm not pregnant, but…"

"But what?" Ciara anxiously asked.

"Well, I don't know how to put this, but I haven't been feeling too well lately. I've made a terrible mistake, and I can't erase what I've done."

Ciara didn't pay much attention to what Kim was saying because another call was beeping in.

"Hold on, Kim. Someone's on my other line," she interrupted, cutting Kim off in the middle of her sentence. When she clicked back over to Kim, she quickly said, "I'll call you later."

Click!

That was it. Ciara hung up the phone in her face. Kim's eyes were full of tears as she placed the phone back on the receiver. Kim could not understand why *this* was happening to *her*. She didn't want to fight this disease alone, but she had no one to turn to except Ciara, who was preoccupied with her own life and issues. Kim continued to stare at her reflection in the mirror, as she sobbed uncontrollably. She grabbed the bottle of prescription pills and read the instructions on the label. It was easier for her to look at the bottle than it was to look at her own image. Unable to cope, she dropped her head low and contemplated ending all of her sorrows. Her dainty hand slowly crept towards a pair of scissors that was on the sink. She grabbed them and walked slowly into her dark bedroom closet.

Ciara didn't have time to focus on what could have been wrong with Kim before she rudely hung up in her face. She would simply call back later to check on her. Now, her focus was on an airtight game plan that would get things back on track in her marriage. Their date tonight had to be perfect, and she was even willing to pull out a few tricks and put it on

Shawn so he would never think of leaving her or their home again. Ciara loved him that much. She stood on her toes and attempted to shake her booty, as if she were performing in front of him. Mrs. Blackwell was prepared and ready for the night.

By the time eight o'clock finally came around, she was looking and feeling like a million dollars. She had on a nice evening dress that was just right for the occasion. The cream colored dress went well with her skin complexion and make up. She had on just enough Vera Wang perfume for Shawn to notice. Her matching purse and heels completed her look. The Motions perm and flat iron gave her hair that magazine look, and the heavy layer of lip gloss gave her lips a wet, sexy look.

If Shawn doesn't want me tonight, I know someone will, because I'm looking too damn good.

"Crazy in Love" by Beyoncé began to play on Ciara's phone. That was the ringtone she had assigned to Shawn for whenever he called her.

"Hello."

"Hey, baby, I'm outside."

"Okay, I'm on my way out." The sound of his voice made her insides flutter and her southern lips quiver.

"Damn, she's looking good. I need me some of that tonight," Shawn said, before she reached the car. His mouth had dropped open as soon as she walked out of the front door.

Ciara was wearing the hell out of that dress. Every curve of her body was accentuated in the right way. He took note and placed his hand on his lap.

It seemed as though time had frozen when Ciara turned around to lock the door. Her dress was so tight that you could see that she didn't have on any panties. Trying to be too smooth, she almost tripped while entering the car.

"Are you okay?" Shawn asked in a joking way.

Steven Morgan

"I'm okay. Thanks for asking. I did almost bust my shit, though."

They started to laugh.

"I miss you, baby. Give me a hug."

As they embraced, a car slowly pulled up beside them.

"Who is that, Shawn?"

The all-black undercover car came to a halt, while Shawn and Ciara continued to observe.

"How are you doing, officer? Is there a problem?"

"No, I just got a report that a homeless man named Toby Jenkins has been harassing people in the neighborhood. Have you two noticed anything?"

Shawn clinched his fist. "No, officer, we haven't seen anyone."

The officer noticed Shawn's reaction, but didn't think too much of it. "Okay, you two have a good night."

"Why is Toby out here harassing people? I think he needs to get some help with his drug problem."

"Let's not talk about Toby right now. You look real nice, and I'm really feeling that dress, baby."

"Thank you, and so do you."

After Shawn turned on the air conditioner, his Perry Ellis cologne permeated the air throughout the car. His navy blue Evisu polo shirt went well with his sharply creased Evisu jeans. Not to mention the fresh navy blue and white Air Max he was wearing with the outfit. To top it off, he had a fresh razor lining.

"Damn, I want to fuck you, baby," Ciara softly mumbled, caught up in her thoughts.

"What did you say?"

"Oh nothing. I just said damn, what the fuck. It's cold in here."

"I'm sorry, sweetheart. I'll cut the air off."

Shawn decided to take Ciara out of the city to the suburbs. They pulled up to Cheeseburger Paradise in Downers Grove. At first, she was upset, but that emotion quickly faded. She knew her husband was tight with money.

As they both got out of the car, Shawn spotted a familiar face. "Isn't that your little boyfriend over there?"

"What? Who are you talking about, babe?" she asked, while looking in the direction of where his eyes were focused.

"Adrian. He's right there with all of them K-town dudes."

"Whatever. You know he use to fuck with Kim."

"Yeah, I know that, but he really wanted you. I don't know how many times he disrespected me because of you."

Adrian was in front of the restaurant leaning on his champagne colored Range Rover with his workers from the block. He was a hustler from around the way that used his money as bait to try to take Ciara away from Shawn. However, she didn't pay him any attention because he was notorious for telling his personal business too much. He told everyone about how he made Kim get naked and dance for him and his little brother. Kim never denied the rumors because she wasn't sure what happened the night she was with Adrian and his little brother. All she remembered was that she popped two X pills and woke up the next morning with cottonmouth.

Adrian spotted Shawn and Ciara getting out of the car as he folded up a knot of fifty-dollar bills in his hand.

"What's up, fam? Do you need some extra money for your meal tonight? I know you making plenty of money at Footlocker, but I thought I should ask you anyway."

The group of guys standing with Adrian started laughing.

Steven Morgan

"Come on, Ciara. Let's go somewhere else," Shawn demanded.

"Go somewhere else? How you gonna let him talk to you like that?"

"Because I'm a boss, shorty. That's why!" Adrian quickly answered.

"A boss? Please! Nobody wants your sorry ass!"

"Nobody, Ciara? What about Kim? I guess you calling your girl a nobody now."

"No, motherfucker, I don't want your ass! That's what I'm saying!"

"Ciara, my Wednesday bitch looks way better than your stuck-up ass. Maybe I can fit you in on Sundays if you act right."

"Fuck you and all your little tramps!" Ciara wrathfully rebutted.

"Hold on, shorty. Calm down before I slap the shit out of you! I know you look good and all, but don't act like you and your man can't get it tonight."

Hearing those words, one of Adrian's workers cocked his gun, as if on cue.

"Shawn, did you hear what he just said to me?"

Ciara was ready for her and Shawn to die after that comment Adrian just made. Ignoring her, Shawn retreated back towards the car.

"Yeah, take y'all lame asses home! Skedaddle you broke motherfuckers!" Adrian made a mockery out of them, while holding onto his diamond-filled charm.

"Fuck you, Adrian! That's fucked up, Shawn! How are you gonna let him talk to your wife like that?"

"I don't want to get into it with them fools tonight. I'm just trying to do us. Just leave it alone, Ciara! I'm trying to have a good night.”

Ciara’s respect for Shawn was headed down the drain. She started to view him in a different light. However, she was willing to let it slide for now since other than their encounter with Adrian, things appeared to be going well. The dysfunctional pair decided to head to another location so they could finish their date in peace.

“Shawn, I’m really having a good time tonight.”

“Me too, and I hope we’re finally on the same page. How about we finish the night on a good note?”

Ciara didn’t hesitate to agree. As she placed Shawn’s hand on her ass, she kissed him passionately. In her mind, Navy Pier turned into a bedroom.

“Slow down a little bit. We can’t get down like this out here,” Shawn said, nervously looking around.

“But I want you right now. I don’t have on any panties, baby.”

“I got us a room down here already.”

“Oh, so you had this planned out?”

“No, I got the room just in case we got too drunk.”

They left Navy Pier and headed to the hotel room Shawn had reserved. As they walked into the room, he pushed her to the bed, lifted her dress above her waist as she bent over, and slid into her warm vagina. He then gave her what she had been longing for…long, hard strokes.

“Damn, boy, you’re trying to kill me.”

Ciara attempted to brace herself with each stroke, while Shawn placed one of his legs on the bed and left the other one remaining on the floor.

“That’s how I like it, baby. Take this pussy. It’s all yours, daddy!”

Shawn continued to lay the pipe like a dude fresh out of

prison. He flipped her over and then went into overdrive as he felt himself reaching his peak. He tried to hold his nut a few seconds longer, but the powerful orgasm rushed through his penis to its tip. After climaxing, his knees felt weak. He slowly walked into the bathroom, trying to stop his children from dripping on the floor.

"Are you okay in there?"

"Yeah, I'm cool."

Ciara felt that she and Shawn were complete again. "So when are you going to move your things back in?" she asked.

She leaned over to retrieve her purse and grabbed a cigar out of the side pocket.

"I thought you only smoked when you're stressed?" he said when he returned to the side of the bed.

"Forget about that. Answer my question. When are you moving back in?"

"What are you talking about? I thought we had an understanding at dinner."

"Wait, what are you talking about?"

"I told you that we will continue to have an open relationship until we can come to some type of agreement in our relationship."

"No, that wasn't the fucking deal, Shawn!" Ciara replied furiously.

"I told you that I'm still in love with Pink and I need some time to think about what I'm going to do."

"Some time? What the hell! You just got some ass and now it's back to that bitch? You make me fucking sick. I can't believe you're still on the same shit!"

"I'm not. I asked if you understood our deal."

Ciara's heart fell to her feet. "I have to go! I can't take this right now! I feel so dumb!"

She grabbed her belongings and her pride and left the room in a hurry. With hurt in her eyes, Ciara stopped to turn and look at the hotel room door. Part of her looked because she could not believe what had just taken place, and the other part of her wanted to see if Shawn was coming behind her to call her back. The door was closed and there was no Shawn. She stepped onto the elevator and pressed the down button.

chapter 6

"Pink, why weren't you answering your phone last night? Why every time I call your phone goes to voicemail? Either you're messing around with another dude, or you just don't want to be bothered with me."

Pink sighed before answering. "I told you I had to work late, Shawn."

"Oh, so every night you're working late now? And every time I call you're either on the other line or your battery is dead?"

"What sense does it make for me to lie about a battery being dead? Either you're going to believe me or you're not. I can't believe you even would come at me like this over a damn cell phone battery?"

Pink couldn't understand why Shawn was giving her such a hard time.

My mother always told me when a man starts pointing pinkies he's usually the one up to no good, she thought, while staring up at her ceiling and waiting on Major Shawn to stop bitching at her.

"I just feel like we're not moving forward in our relationship. It's like we're heading in two different directions. I'm starting to question how serious you are about us."

The phone was quiet for about three seconds, and in that

time, Shawn began to see this new love situation in a new light. He felt more like her father than her man. She always had an excuse for this and a reason for that. His line of questioning was starting to wear thin on him. He was doing everything to Pink that Ciara did to annoy the hell out of him in their marriage. Still, he couldn't stop wondering if Pink's mind and heart was in it.

"Hello! I guess you don't have nothing to say now, do you?"

"Sweetie, I really don't have time for this. I have to get ready to perform tonight, and I don't even know what routine I'm going to do. Can we please talk about this later?"

"It's always later with you, Pink! I'm always pushed to the bottom of your fucking list! I thought you weren't working tonight? And I hope Lisa's malnutrition ass isn't your partner either, because you're not going to make any money tonight."

"First of all, Lisa's my girl and she's a true hustler! Thank you very much. And besides, she started me in this business. What do you have to say about that, college boy?"

Pink definitely pissed Shawn off with that last comment.

"What the hell is that suppose to mean? You think I'm a lame or something? I'm just trying to look out for you. Lisa isn't your friend, and she isn't a go-getter. Ha!" Shawn laughed as if that was going to hurt Pink's feelings. "Okay, since that's your best friend and all, who did she say helped her steal the clothes out of Tops and Bottoms last summer?"

"Me, but she only told because she was scared."

"Damn that! You didn't even have anything to do with it."

"I know, but she's still my girl, and that's that."

"Well, your buddy left you like Prince's Pants.

"What do you mean, Prince's Pants?"

"She left you ass-out."

Pink began to laugh as she closed the bag of chips, grabbed her towel off the foot of the bed, and walked towards the bathroom to take a steamy, hot shower. She needed to relax after this draining conversation with Shawn.

"Shawn, can we continue this conversation later on when I come home?"

"Yeah, whatever!" Shawn sarcastically said, then pressed the end button.

******

"I can't believe Shawn's ass. I don't know what to say, Ciara, because he's gone too far with this now."

"I know, but I think it's time for me to go on with my life. I'm just so hurt. I didn't know Shawn was serious about this whole situation. I know we had our bad times, but I didn't think he was falling out of love with me."

"I don't think he doesn't love you. I think he just doesn't know what he wants right now. I know what we should do."

"What should we do?"

"I think we should go…"

Before Kim could finish her sentence, Ciara cut her off because someone was banging on the door.

"Kim, I'm going to have to call you back. Someone's at my door."

"Okay, but make sure you call back, because I really have to talk to you about something."

"I will," Ciara said, rushing Kim off the phone.

Ciara couldn't get down the stairs fast enough. Her long black hair bounced behind her, as she almost missed a step and fell face first.

Who in the hell is it banging like the damn feds? I hope this is Pink, because I got something for her ass this time!

Ciara looked through the peephole and saw a slim man standing in front of her door.

"Yes, who is it?"

"Hi, is Ciara home?" the slender man replied.

"Who wants to know?"

"You don't know me, but I think we need to talk about Shawn and my wife, Patrice," he lied.

Ciara was about to open the door until he mentioned Shawn's name and she realized she was home alone. Without warning, she ran back up the stairs and grabbed her all-black .25 caliber Lorcin from under the mattress. She took the safety lock off and headed back downstairs. She opened the door slowly, with the gun visible enough so the man standing there could see it. Frightened, he took a step back from the doorway.

"Sweet Jesus! Please don't shoot me!" the guy pleaded.

"I don't know you and I don't trust you. Now, all three of us can talk, or I'll just let one of us talk. It's your call," she said, referring to her gun.

"I'll explain everything as soon as you put that gun down. Just the sight of it makes me weak in the knees."

"No, I think me and old Leroy here would like to listen to what you have to say together."

"Okay, but can I at least come in then?"

Ciara directed the man towards a chair that was only a couple of feet from the front door. While keeping an eye on her gun, the man slowly walked in.

"I know that I came over here unannounced, but girl, we really need to talk about this bullshit that's going on. My name is Byron, and I'm Patrice's husband. Patrice has been having an affair with your husband for about three or four months now. "

Before Byron could finish his sentence, Ciara interrupted him.

"Who in the hell is Patrice, and what does she have to do with me?" she quickly asked, waving the gun.

He appeared to be too nervous to talk.

"Ciara, I'll feel much more comfortable if you would put that gun away," Byron said.

"At this point, I don't give a shit how you feel. Just tell me about Shawn and this bitch Patricia, or whatever her name is!"

"Her name is Patrice, and she strips at Club Cowboys on the south side. You might know her by her stage name, Pink. We've been married for two years and she's been cheating on me since day one. I guess her and Shawn met while she was at work. At first, I thought it was just another one of her flings and it would be over, but she told me that she wanted a divorce so she could start a new life with him. I didn't want to believe it, but I knew it was serious when I followed them to the Seneca Hotel the other night. I've tried to be there for her when she needed me, but I guess that wasn't enough."

Ciara was flabbergasted and confused.

"I wish it wasn't true, but it is, Ciara."

"But how do you know about me and where I live?"

"I became somewhat of an investigator with this situation. I was so hurt about Patrice wanting a divorce, I found myself following her and Shawn every day. I found out about you from this crackhead that I saw talking to you the other day," Byron replied, as he crossed his legs.

It was something about Byron that gave Ciara a perturbed feeling. It was like he was out of place with himself or didn't belong. Byron was very much in touch with his feminine side. Besides the crossing of the legs displaying a womanly gesture, he wore a Juicy Couture outfit with the matching Juicy Couture backpack. Ciara wondered how this man even had a wife. His tight-ass pants and mannerism probably forced her to cheat.

"Well, I'm not going to sit here and talk all night. I just needed to get some stuff off of my chest. I hope I didn't upset you, but I felt that you should know the truth about what was going on. I'm sorry for disturbing you like this."

"No, I'm glad you came over here. I really appreciate it, Byron. Shawn and I are separated at the present time. I don't know what the future holds for us, but I do know that I'm here for him no matter what. Do you have a number where I can reach you?"

Byron couldn't believe Ciara, as he stared at her with revulsion. He slightly threw a business card at her before walking out of the door with an attitude.

After closing the door, she looked at the business card. "Hair R Us" read above Byron's name and phone number. Upon returning to the living room, she called Kim.

Meanwhile, Byron got in his car and lit a cigarette, while staring at Ciara's front door. He twirled the cigarette between his fingers before placing it between his pout lips. He was ready for payback.

"I'll show his ass for hitting on me. After all of the embarrassment and lies, this is how you play me, Shawn? Fuck you!" Byron said, as he started the car and pulled off.

******

"Ciara, let me call you back. I'm trying to do something."

"You're so nasty. Is Eric over there?"

"No, I'm trying to take this medicine. I'll explain

everything when I call back."

Kim hung up the phone and placed the bottle of medication on the bathroom counter. She slowly stepped into the shower with a bottle of Caress body wash and a face towel.

Still, the hot water from the shower couldn't stop the tears from falling down her face. Kim's days of unsafe sex and fun had finally caught up to her. The severity of her lifestyle was high, but she never imagined she would be facing HIV. She didn't have time to think of that consequence when she was in the middle of wild, paid-for sex.

Kim stood there immobile. As the water from the shower ran down her body, she wanted her troubles to be released from her system and follow the water down the drain. She quietly said a heartfelt prayer to God and wished on any star possible, but it was far too late. The damage had been done, and she would just have to find a way to live the rest of her adult life as healthy as possible with the disease.

As Kim turned the shower knob slowly to the off position, she could hear her phone ringing, but by the time she grabbed the towel, it had stopped. Looking at the phone's display screen, she saw it had been Ciara calling again.

I just told her that I'd call her back. Why is she calling me again?

Her phone rang once again.

Now what the hell does he fucking want? The sight of Shawn's name on her phone made her sick to the stomach. She picked up the phone and talked to him for what she hoped would be the last time.

"I don't want anything else to do with your dirty ass. I told you to stop calling me, Shawn!" she yelled into the phone after answering. "What we did was a one-time thing! I feel bad about it as it is. I hate you, and I don't want anything to do with your conniving ass!"

"You gave me something, bitch! I knew I shouldn't have touched your nasty ass."

"I didn't give you anything! I was clean before me and you hooked up. I told you to wear a damn condom, but you were too drunk to listen!"

"You seduced me, Kim! I told you that I was drunk, but you still started sucking my dick. I was inebriated and you took advantage of that."

"I didn't do anything that you didn't want to happen. We're both to blame. You're a grown man, and you knew exactly what you were doing."

"Well, when I catch you, you're going to wish we never met."

"Is that a threat, Shawn?"

"It's more like a promise."

"Keep on with the threats and I'll tell Ciara everything!"

"Tell her what? Do you really think she'll believe you over her husband?"

"Her husband? Nigga, please! You're old news. Ciara has someone that cares about her now. You can take your broke ass back to that nasty-ass stripper and live unhappily ever after. The bad thing is that I warned Ciara about your no-good ass!"

"Whatever you say, Kim, but I know the fucking truth. Just watch your back, bitch!"

With that, Shawn hung up the phone.

In a rage, Kim threw the cordless phone across the room. "I hate that bastard!"

She grabbed her sky blue jogging suit off the couch by the fish tank, and after finding her car keys, she left out the door, jumped in her car, and peeled off like she was in the Indy 500. As she scanned through the radio stations, the only decent song on was Kelly Price's "A Friend of Mine".

"I really messed up," Kim said softly to herself, as she turned the radio off.

When she pulled into the Marathon gas station by her apartment, she saw Toby sitting on the curb. It must have been the medicine making her nicer, because she actually felt like talking to him today.

"What's the matter, Toby?"

"I don't know what to do with myself. I'm nothing, just a damn nobody!"

"What happened? Why are you so down on yourself?"

"You know you don't care about me and my bullshit."

"Don't be like that, Toby. Tell me what's wrong."

"I just lost my best friend Chris in these streets."

"I'm so sorry to hear that, Toby. How did he die?"

"Die! He didn't die. The damn fool just got locked up for stealing. I was looking for him this morning and someone told me that he was locked up." Toby took a deep breath. "I think I need to get away for a while and figure out what I'm going to do with myself out here. You know? Life on these streets is lonely. Sometimes I wake up thinking it will be my last day on earf."

"Last day on what?" Kim asked, unsure of what Toby said.

"On earf…earf. You heard what I said."

Damn, he does look terrible, Kim thought.

Toby looked like an old-ass dust mop sitting on the curb. He had on a filthy Taste of Chicago t-shirt that was at least three sizes too big for him. His pants were full of stains and holes. To be honest, he looked just like how Kim felt inside, terrible.

"Besides, if Shawn finds out where I'm at, he'll kill me.

I can't run forever." Toby started shaking his head in disbelief. "He's blaming me for something he did. What's going to happen is out of my control."

"Shawn? Why would he want to kill you?"

"If I told you, you probably wouldn't believe me anyway," Toby replied, as he began to walk away from Kim.

"No, tell me what's wrong. Do you have some beef with Shawn?"

"Promise me that you won't say anything to Ciara," Toby begged.

"I promise. Cross my heart and hope to die. What happened between y'all?"

"One night, I was trying to hustle up some money and saw Shawn's car parked on this dark block. I went up to the window, and he was in the car with some pretty-boy-looking dude who was taking care of him. You know, taking…care of…him," Toby slowly repeated.

"So what? What's the big deal about that?"

Toby turned his head away from Kim and took a deep breath.   "Kim, the man was giving Shawn head! I mean, he was going to work on your boy Shawn. Yes, don't give me that look. I'm talking about Shawn Blackwell!"

"What? Are you serious, Toby?" Kim screamed.

"I promise to God that Shawn was in the car with another man. The shit freaked me out, girl."

"I know it did. I always had a feeling that Shawn had those types of tendencies, but I couldn't gather enough nerve to tell Ciara about it."

"Now, I'm scared for my life. For the last couple of days, Shawn's been following me."

"Well, that's kind of deep. Why don't you go to the police? If you feel that your life is in danger, you should tell someone with authority."

Toby began to unscrew the cap off of a bottle that he had covered with a brown paper bag. He took two gulps of the liquor, then wiped his mouth before answering her.

"Because I ain't a snitch, woman!"

"A snitch! Are you crazy?"

"I know, but I don't know what else to do. I live on the streets, and I don't want to die in them."

Toby could feel a nervous lump in his throat as he swallowed. The strong liquor burning his esophagus as it went down didn't even help calm his nerves.

"Well, if you feel like that, I don't think it's safe for you to be on the streets either. I don't understand why you're so afraid. Shit, Shawn is a soft-ass baby. He isn't about to do anything!"

"Well, can I come and stay with you for a couple of days?"

"Hell no! I don't think that would be a good idea."

"Yeah, I know, because I'll probably end up stealing all of your shit," Toby replied with sarcasm. "Alright then, I'll catch you later. Stay up."

Kim nodded her head and walked into the convenience store.

"Hey Kim, wait a minute. Do you have a couple dollars I can borrow?"

Kim scrambled through her purse and handed Toby seven dollars.

"Damn, you pay more than Taco Bell do," Toby replied, as he quickly folded the money.

"You're too crazy for me, Toby."

Chapter 7

The next morning, Ciara woke up to a couple arguing outside of the window. *Damn, that sounds like Shawn and me out there fighting,* Ciara thought, while yawning. She was off to a sluggish start this morning, but it was nothing that couldn't be cured with some green motivation medicine.

Ciara finally rolled out of the bed and walked towards her dresser, with her ass bouncing in the hot pink pajama pants. Her nipples were hard because of the cold floor in the bedroom, and she was looking like a five-star chick early in the morning. There weren't too many men in America that wouldn't want to witness that scene every morning. A camera and baby oil is all that was needed to complete a sexy scene.

After grabbing the remote and the ashtray that held her peach-flavored Swisher, Ciara broke open the cigar slowly with her fingernail and dumped the tobacco into the ashtray. Once her motivation medicine was rolled, she headed downstairs to enjoy her session in the dining room. Sitting at the table and sorting through the mail from the previous day, she came across Shawn's cell phone bill.

To her surprise, it was a bill from Nextel, which she had no clue Shawn owned. Ciara couldn't wait to find Pink's number on there so she could call and tell that stripping heifer to go straight to hell. She quickly tore through the envelope, almost breaking her fingernail. Scanning through the bill, she noticed three repeated phone numbers. The first number she recognized as Eric's number, but her eyes nearly bulged out of

Steven Morgan

the sockets when she noticed the next number. It belonged to her best friend, Kim.

Ciara dropped the mail, grabbed her cell phone out of her purse, and quickly dialed Kim's number. Upset and in a rush, she dialed the wrong number.

"Hi, this is Popeye's. How can I help you?"

I'm really trippin', Ciara thought as she hung up. *I can't believe this bitch Kim!* She was beyond being pissed off, as she finally was able to dial the correct number.

"Hey Ciara, what's up?" Kim confidently answered.

"Bitch, your ass is what's up."

"What? What are you talking about?"

"Bitch, I just read Shawn's cell phone bill and your number was on there like twenty times! You've been fucking my man! How could you play me like this?"

"Wait, Ciara! Please let me explain what happened."

"No, fuck that! I'm going to kill you when I catch you, bitch! You fucking homewrecker!"

Oh my goodness! What am I going to do? Kim couldn't think. Her mind was racing at one hundred miles per hour. *I have to leave this house and get a room somewhere for a couple of days until I can at least talk to Ciara and tell her what happened,* Kim thought, while frantically pacing the floor in her small bedroom.

Quickly, she grabbed her purse and some clothes out of the bedroom closet, and ran out of the house. About fifteen minutes later, Ciara drove up and jumped out of the car fuming. She didn't even bother to put the car into park, because she had driven up on the curb and into the bushes when she pulled up.

"Bitch, open this motherfucking door! I'm gonna kill you, hoe!" Ciara vigorously kicked Kim's front door.

Boom! Boom! Boom!

"Hey, what the hell is wrong with you?" the next-door neighbor screamed at Ciara.

"Mind your fucking business before I come over there and beat your old ass, lady!"

The lady couldn't believe what Ciara just said to her.

"Well, you first have to get past this army that I got over here, you little whore!"

She must have fell and bumped her damn head, Ciara thought. "Bitch, who in the hell are you calling a whore, with your old ass? I'll beat you and your army's ass."

Ciara started to walk toward the neighbor's door, but stopped when she noticed the old lady was holding a small handgun.

"You know what, old lady? I don't have time for dumb shit!" Ciara said, as she slowly began to walk backwards, hoping the old lady didn't have a slavery flashback and start shooting.

As Ciara started to walk back towards Kim's house, she grabbed a brick that was lying in the garden and threw it through Kim's front window. It didn't stop right there, because Ciara drew back and threw another brick through a different window.

"That's enough! You have to leave!"

Ciara waved her middle finger to the old woman, while hocking up a glob of spit for Kim's front door. After leaving her mark, she jumped into her car and peeled off.

She felt like she didn't have anything else to lose. Her husband's punk ass left her for a stripper, and to add insult to injury, she found out her best friend since childhood slept with him, too. In Ciara's mind, all three of them could take turns kissing her black, plump ass before they headed straight to hell.

Preoccupied with thoughts of whooping ass, she drove through a red light near her house.

"Here we go," Ciara said, when she noticed a police car speeding up behind her with its lights and siren on.

She flipped on her turn signal and began to pull over slowly

Steven Morgan

while wiping tears from her face. However, the police weren't even thinking about Ciara. They flew by at top speed. Just to be on the safe side, she fastened her seatbelt and drove five miles below the speed limit all the way back home. When she made it there, she started calling everybody that she thought knew Kim. She even attempted to call Shawn several times, but he wasn't answering the phone.

"This ya boy Shawn. Leave a message."

"Bitch nigga, when I see you, I'm going to stomp a hole in your ass! I just found out about you and that hoe Kim. I hope you die, motherfucker!"

Ciara hung up the phone praying Shawn would have the audacity to call her back. At this point, she couldn't think, and the longer it took for her to get a hold of Kim, the more furious her thoughts became. She started to call all of the local hotels. She didn't bother with calling the motels, because she knew Kim wouldn't step foot into a trashy motel. She didn't have any family members to stay with, and wherever Kim was had to be close because she never drove on the expressway. Ciara got a phone book and called every hotel within close proximity.

She scanned down the list of hotels in the Yellow Pages and came across a Holiday Inn located in the western suburbs of Chicago. Coincidentally, it was the same Holiday Inn where Kim would meet Adrian for quickies and overnight visits.

"Hi, this is Mary with Holiday Inn. Will you be making reservations today?" the perky white woman answered.

"Can I please be connected to Kim Morris's room?"

"I'm so sorry, miss, but you're breaking up a little bit and I can't hear you. Did you say Kim Morris or Kim Morton?"

"Uh, Kim Morton," Ciara nervously said.

"Yes, I have it right here. Please hold while I connect you."

"Wait! You don't have to connect me because I'm outside the hotel. I just needed to know which room she's in again."

"Not a problem, miss. She's in room 342. Is there anything else I can help you with, ma'am?"

"No, I'm okay now. Thanks for your help."

"You're welcome, and thank you for calling Holiday Inn."

Dummy, you're not supposed to give out that type of information, Ciara thought as she hung up the phone.

After grabbing her car keys and two Ibuprofens out of the bathroom cabinet, she left. She weaved in and out of the expressway lanes, flooring it to the Holiday Inn. A small moving van slowed her up, but she was lucky because a state trooper was about 200 yards up the road. So, she reduced her speed and buckled up quickly.

His ass may have to follow me, because Kim is going to need some medical, state, and federal help when I catch her ass, Ciara thought, while adjusting her rearview mirror.

She drove in silence with tears in her eyes, as The Game's CD blasted through the Nissan's factory speakers. The only thing on her mind was Kim and her exit to the Holiday Inn.

About thirty minutes later, Ciara finally made it to the hotel's exit. It was show time, but this wasn't the Apollo. Ciara drove around looking for Kim's car and came upon it parked next to the hotel's dumpster.

Ciara didn't bother wasting any time as she swallowed the two Ibuprofens in an attempt to lessen any future pain she might feel from scrapping with Kim. Then she scampered through the parking lot towards the hotel lobby. As she started to walk down the hall, the young girl at the front desk stopped her in her tracks.

"Hi. May I help you?"

This nosey bitch, Ciara thought. "Yes, as a matter of fact you can. I seemed to have left my key in the room, and I was wondering if you could give me another one."

"Yes, no problem. What's your name and room number

Steven Morgan
again?"

"It's Kim Morton, and I'm in room 342."

"May I please see your ID, Ms. Morton?" the clerk sarcastically said.

Ciara hesitated for a second because she knew the young clerk was on some bullshit.

"Yeah, sure, give me a second," Ciara replied, while pretending to search through her pants pockets. "It must be locked in the room with the rest of my things. I'll bring it right down to show you."

"Never mind, I'll take your word for it this time, Ms. Morton. Is everything okay?" the clerk asked with a concerned look on her face, as she handed Ciara the room key.

Ciara didn't bother to answer or wait for the slow elevator. Instead, she took the stairs. After she reached the third floor, she had to take a break because she was winded. After a few moments, she slowly walked down the hallway looking at the room numbers. Kim's room was only three doors away from the staircase. She didn't want to make a scene until she physically got to Kim, so she decided to knock quietly on the door with her finger over the peephole. After a couple of knocks, Ciara opened the door with the key card. She walked into the room and heard the sound of the shower running. She stepped over a brand-new pair of thongs that Kim left on the floor by the door.

Fucking slut! I need to find her keys, because she might try to run on me.

As soon as the thought crossed Ciara's mind, she heard the shower cut off. She couldn't control herself as she ran into the bathroom after Kim.

"Bitch!" Ciara yelled, taking a swing at Kim's head.

Trying to avoid Ciara's barrage of punches, Kim fell back into the shower.

"Stop! Please stop!" Kim screamed, as Ciara started to stomp her. She tried to guard herself, but Ciara had her at a major disadvantage in the slippery shower.

"Bitch, I told you before don't fuck with my man! You're just like all these other petty hoes out here! I trusted you with my life, you fucking slut!" Ciara was enraged.

Kim's torso was covered with bruises and Air Max footprints. She continued to scream, but her cries went unheard.

"I didn't mess with Shawn! He tried to sleep with me!"

"Bitch, stop lying! I saw your phone number on his fucking phone bill."

Ciara stepped out the shower, ripped the shower curtain rod from the wall, and started hitting Kim across her wet body. The impact from the rod left red marks on Kim's face and arms. Exhausted, Ciara dropped the shower rod on top of Kim's motionless body and ran out of the hotel room.

"I don't give a fuck anymore! Wait until I catch up with Shawn and Pink's nasty ass! It's just me against the world now!" Ciara yelled, while removing her bloody shirt and throwing it in the dumpster next to Kim's car. She then jumped into her car wearing nothing but jeans and a bra and headed back home.

The next morning, the housekeeper came in to clean Kim's room.

"Hello, it's housekeeping with fresh towels and sheets. Hello! Is anyone in here?" the older Hispanic lady called out with her heavy accent. As she proceeded to enter the room, she saw Kim lying in the shower still unconscious, but breathing.

"Oh my God!" the lady fearfully screamed, as she rushed to the phone and dialed 9-1-1.

******

At the hospital, Kim was in serious condition with a broken jaw and other minor injuries. Her left eye was swollen shut and her head was covered with bandages. Bruises and welts

Steven Morgan

covered a large portion of her torso and arms. Kim was being fed through an IV bag, and the medication being allotted to her was not stopping the agonizing pain she was feeling. As soon as she began to feel the affect from the Norco pain pill, two detectives came in the room to question her about what happened to her the night before.

"Good evening, Ms. Morton. I'm Detective Peter Abbott, and I just wanted to ask you a couple of questions about what happened to you. I understand you have a broken jaw from the incident, so I'm going to ask you to write down your responses on this notepad. Do you know who did this to you and perhaps the person's whereabouts?"

Kim looked strangely at both of the detectives. Then she slowly sat up in the bed, grabbed the pad out of the detective's hand, and started to write. She wrote down a name and address on the pad and handed it back to the detective.

"Are you sure, Ms. Morton," the detective suspiciously asked.

Kim shook her head yes.

"Okay, thank you. Try to relax and I hope you feel better," the detective replied, as he placed two checkmarks next to the name of the person Kim wrote down.

"Let's go, Ralph. I know exactly where these apartments are."

About an hour later, three police cars drove into the Buckingham apartment complex at full speed. It only took a few minutes for the police to find the address they were looking for. The police cars came to a sudden stop and the officers jumped out with their guns drawn and warrant papers in hand.

"Open the fucking door! We have a warrant for Shawn Blackwell!"

"What!" Shawn yelled, as he tried to grab some pants to put on.

"Who is that?" Pink asked.

"Just go and lay down. Let me handle this!"

Boom! Boom!

"Stop banging on my fucking door! What seems to be the problem?" Shawn said, as he quickly swung open the door.

"We have a warrant for your arrest, Mr. Blackwell," the police officer said in a vulgar manner, while handing Shawn the warrant.

"For what? What the hell did I do?" Shawn cried, as the officers swiftly placed him in handcuffs.

"Stop! What are you doing to him? What did he do?"

"Pink, just call my lawyer and Eric! You bitches need to tell me what's going on!" Shawn screamed, as the officers directed him towards the patrol car.

One of the officers gave him an open hand slap to the back of his neck. "You're the only bitch out here. You like to hit on women? You're a pussy and a stupid nigger!"

"Take me out of these handcuffs and I'll show you who's a pussy, white boy!"

Shawn continued to argue with the officers all the way to the police station. He was nervous and didn't know exactly what was going on. A million things were running through his mind as the officers drove him down to the entrance where booking and fingerprinting was done. Inside the police station, he was placed in a holding room for about six hours before anyone spoke with him. Two detectives walked into the dark, urine-smelling interrogation room where he was handcuffed to a chair.

"How are you doing, Mr. Blackwell?" one detective asked, while pulling out a pack of Newports and offering one to Shawn.

"I don't want your faggot-ass cigarette. Just tell me what's going on and when I can leave."

The tall, stout detective stood up and looked Shawn directly in the face. "So you don't have any idea why we have you down here at the station, Shawn?"

"No, I fucking don't!" Shawn said in a loud voice.

"There's no need to yell at us, Shawn. We didn't make you hit that woman!" the officer replied in a sarcastic way.

"What the hell are you talking about? Like I told those two assholes that brought me in, I didn't hit anybody!"

"What about Kim Morton? Does that name ring a bell, you fucker? We found her severely beaten and unconscious in a hotel room last night."

"And? What the fuck does that have to do with me? I don't even know who Kim Morton is!"

"She named you as her attacker, you pussy!" the detective yelled, as he grabbed Shawn's collar and pushed his head to the table vigorously.

"Calm down, Chuck! If he doesn't want to cooperate with us, it's okay, because we'll nail his black ass sooner or later. He's not worth it," the other detective said, while trying his best to calm his upset partner.

"I didn't hit or hurt anyone! You must have the wrong guy. I want to call my lawyer," Shawn begged, as he tried to stand up.

"I need you to have a seat, Mr. Blackwell," the detective demanded.

The irate detective grabbed his partially lit cigarette and walked out of the room with the other detective.

Who in the hell beat Kim up? I know I didn't do anything to her. I hope Eric and Pink are on their way to get me out of this piece of shit place, Shawn thought, placing his head down on the table.

Moments later, another officer came into the room and granted Shawn his phone privileges.

******

Kim was required to stay an additional three days at the hospital because of the swelling to her head and jaw. For the next couple of days, she was only able to receive food through an IV bag. However, she was allowed to put ice on her lips to prevent them from chapping. She was able to see a little better through her bruised left eye because the swelling had subsided. Her body was extremely sore, but she was able to walk around her room with the assistance of the nurses who cared for her. Sure, she was in bad shape, but she couldn't possibly feel as bad as Ciara felt when she found out about her and Shawn creeping behind her back.

Kim had gotten herself into a lot of trouble. Shawn hated her. Ciara wanted to kill her and *actually* tried to kill her. She truly believed she was finally paying the price for crossing too many lines.

She heard a soft knock on her door. Unable to talk, she pressed the nurse button on the remote. For some reason, the nurse didn't respond to her page, though. The doorknob began to slowly turn, and Kim's heart started to race as she sat up in the bed. She didn't know who was coming in, but the last person she wanted to catch her defenseless was Ciara. Kim's heart began to slow down when she saw Eric and a nurse walk through the door. Her eyes were open wide, like she had just seen a poltergeist.

Why is Eric here? Kim thought to herself.

"Is everything okay, Ms. Morton?" the nurse asked, while walking over to Kim's bed.

Kim shook her head yes.

"Okay, just buzz me again if you need anything else."

Eric grabbed a chair that was near her bed and sat down.

"I know you can't talk, but I just came by to see how you were doing. Damn, I thought your last name was Morris?"

Kim just looked at Eric as if he hadn't said one word. He thought it was strange of Kim not to respond to him.

Steven Morgan

"Anyway, I heard your name over the dispatch the other night when they brought you in. Here, I bought you some flowers and a card," he said, while placing the card and flowers on a small table near Kim, who didn't even take the time to look at the items.

"So, how are you feeling?"

Kim raised her hand and gave Eric a thumbs-up.

"I'm sorry this happened to you. First, you're in the hospital, and then Pink called and told me that Shawn got arrested. I tried to find out where he is, but I don't think his name is in the system yet."

Kim slowly reached for the pen and pad that was next to the flowers on the stand and began to write. Once she finished writing, she handed the paper to Eric. He looked at the paper that had two questions on it.

Does Shawn know I'm in this hospital?

"No, I just told you I haven't heard from Shawn. Why?" Eric asked with an uneasy look on his face.

Kim pointed to the pad at the next question.

Can you please leave? And thank you for the flowers.

"Damn, it's like that? Well, take care, bitch! I show you some love by coming all the way up here to see you and I get treated like shit. I hope whoever beat your ass comes and puts their other foot in your ass, bitch!" Eric said, as he balled up the piece of paper and threw it in her face.

He walked toward the door, looked back at Kim who was still calmly lying in bed, and yelled, "Good riddance!" Then he slammed the door behind him as he left out.

I have to leave this place before Ciara and Shawn finds out that I'm here, Kim thought, as she reached for the remote to page the nurse. She repeatedly pressed the nurse button for about three seconds or so until the nurse came rushing in to see what was wrong with her. Kim was already in the process of writing on another sheet of paper when the nurse stormed in.

She quickly finished what she was writing and handed the piece of paper to the nurse.

Please transfer me to another room. I don't feel safe here. I think I'm in danger!

The nurse didn't question her because she could see the seriousness in Kim's eyes. Instead, the nurse left the room, and about ten minutes later, two transporters came to move Kim into another room in the hospital.

Kim remained there and was released two weeks later. In all honesty, Kim didn't know what to do after she was released.

She had one of her flunky male friends take her to the hotel so she could get her car. On the way, Kim had a million and one thoughts racing through her head. Although her jaw was still healing, she managed to thank her ride when she was dropped off.

"Thank you, God. I thought they were going to tow my car from here," she painfully mumbled to herself.

As she started towards the car, she noticed the back window had a brick through it. Opening the back door, she carefully grabbed the red brick, making sure not to cut herself on the broken glass. The brick had a rubber band and photo attached to it. She removed the rubber band so she could examine the picture closely. It was a picture Ciara took of herself holding up her middle finger. Tears began to form in Kim's eyes as she dropped both the brick and picture on the ground.

While driving home, Kim reflected on everything that had taken place in her life within the last month. She really couldn't get the thought of Shawn being with another man out of her head.

I can't believe Shawn was with another man. Maybe Toby was a little too high that night when he saw Shawn in the car. Another man? Maybe it is true, but I hope it's not, Kim thought, as her stomach began to turn.

Her phone rang, interrupting her thoughts, and it was Ciara. Kim was about to flip open her phone, but realized she couldn't talk. Then she had a quick flashback of the beating that Ciara put on her in the hotel room, and therefore, she decided to send Ciara to the voicemail.

I'm sorry, Ciara, but I'm not in the mood to get cursed out right now. She tossed her cell phone on the passenger seat.

Figuring Ciara had left a crazy voicemail, Kim decided to check it when she stopped at a traffic light.

"One new message received at 11:22 a.m.," the computerized voice announced.

"Bitch, it ain't over! I'm going to fuck you up every day until I die or until I forget about the shit you did to me. So, sleep with one eye open, hoe!"

Kim quickly deleted the message.

This chick is loco. I need my gun permit ASAP.

She adjusted all of her mirrors and carefully surveyed her surroundings while pulling up slowly to another red light.

Chapter 8

"Damn, Pink, that was outstanding! I didn't know you could do it like that," Shawn said, gasping for air.

"I had to show you how much I missed you when you were in jail," she replied, then kissed him softly on his cheek.

"But, baby, I was only locked up for two weeks."

"Yeah, but it felt like two years to me. I still don't understand why you got locked up, though."

"Just leave it alone!"

Not wanting to spark an argument, she rolled off of him and walked into the bathroom.

"Hey," he called out to her, "I've been thinking about this for a while now, and I think we should take our sex life to another level. I want to try some different things. You know, fulfill our fantasies?"

"What do you mean? I don't have any fantasies that need fulfilling," she said, as she exited the bathroom in her birthday suit with her perky nipples standing out from her full breasts.

"Well, first, let me ask you this. Have you ever had a threesome before?"

"Yeah, I've had tons of them," Pink answered in a nonchalant voice.

"What!" Shawn screamed, jumping from the bed.

"Calm down, boy. I'm just playing with you, but it is something I thought about doing before."

"So would you consider doing it with me?"

Steven Morgan

"Yes, baby. I think it'll be a fun and enjoyable experience for the both of us. But I don't want you to get crazy on me and start dipping off on your own with other chicks behind my back."

Not believing what his ears were hearing, he started to smile from ear to ear.

"Hold on, Shawn! I'm not doing it with you and your wife. That's definitely out of the question."

"This has nothing to do with Ciara. This is our thing. I want you to feel special. However, I would like to do this as soon as possible, if you don't mind."

"The sooner the better," she replied, while squeezing toothpaste on her toothbrush.

Pink always wanted to know how another woman felt. Most of all, she wanted to experience what it was like to have her pearl tongue pleased by a beautiful woman. Most of the dancers at the club were bi-sexual and loving it. It seemed like it added an extra dash of spice to their sex life.

At the same time, Shawn was lost in his own thoughts and couldn't wait until everything went down.

******

Ciara was in her bedroom listening to Marvin Gaye while burning up all the pictures she had of Shawn and Kim.

"Damn, I need another bottle of Moet," she said out loud, while looking through the narrow hole of the bottle.

Ding! Ciara dropped the empty bottle on the floor.

"My best friend and my damn husband. All this time and I was too stupid to know. I hate myself for being so gullible. This shit is like some fucked-up dream. I know how to handle this, though. They say the only way to get over somebody is to get under someone else."

Ciara could feel the tunes from Marvin Gaye's song

"What's Going On" in her bones, as she continued to wipe the salty tears from her face. In an attempt to pull herself together, she walked into the bathroom and started the shower. While the water was warming up, she went to her closet to find the shortest, most revealing dress she owned.

"Here it is! It's perfect. It shows too much and covers too little. The first man that I find attractive tonight is coming home with me. I'm going to be a 'Kim' tonight. Oops, I mean a hoe tonight," Ciara said, laughing as she placed the dress on her bed before stumbling towards the bathroom.

After a long shower, mainly to sober up, she was ready for business. Her dress was the perfect fit, and she knew the perfect place to go show it off.

Just a pinch is all I need, Ciara thought, while spraying on some Paris Hilton perfume. After grabbing her purse and keys, she headed out the door. The drive to the club was short and sweet for Ciara because she drove with all the windows down, not caring if the wind messed up her hair. She pulled into the parking lot of the club and slowly looked around at the cars.

"Oh yeah, there's some real ballers out tonight," Ciara said, noticing a fleet of 750 BMW's and other luxury vehicles in the parking lot.

Once she found a space next to a midnight-blue Range Rover, Ciara tried to give herself a quick overview in the rearview mirror, but was distracted by the sound of familiar voices nearby.

Oh my goodness, I know that annoying mouse voice from anywhere. Is that Tasha Franklin, with her loud ass? Ciara thought, while squinting up her eyes at the group of women standing across the parking lot.

"Hey Catherine!" one of the women yelled, not knowing Ciara's real name.

"Hi, and the name is Ciara!"

"That's what I said, Cathy," the intoxicated woman

Steven Morgan
quickly said.

As Ciara got closer to the women, she could smell the alcohol in the air. She didn't respond because she didn't want the women to get riled up and ruin her mission for the night. So, instead, she just smiled and continued to walk towards the front entrance to the club.

"That bitch thinks she looks better than us. Fuck you, hoe!" one woman yelled from the group.

"And she definitely can't hear," Tasha added.

It's cool. I'll catch up with them hoes another time, Ciara thought.

After the overweight bouncers stopped flirting with her, she finally made it inside. It was game time.

She did not want anyone buying her drinks. She did not have any time to stop to talk to anyone. She was there to get her game on. Ciara glanced at a side mirror on the wall by the coat check area and loved what she saw. Then, she walked over to the bar with a sexy, attention-demanding swagger.

"So what will it be?" the bartender asked.

After placing her order, she heard the voice of a male who was standing right behind her.

"I'll have whatever she's having. They don't make them like this anymore. Look at what we have here."

Ciara slowly turned around as the bartender handed her the bottled water.

"That'll be $4.75, ma'am."

"Oh, this one is on me, playa, and you can keep the change," the man said, while handing the bartender five wrinkled dollar bills.

"Thank you, but I have my own money," Ciara voiced, as she unscrewed the cap of the Voss water bottle.

"I can't get a thank you, sweetheart?"

Ciara almost spit her water into the man's face when she noticed what he had on. The overweight shot caller had on a silver and pink sweater, black dress slacks, and a four-finger ring that had "BOSS MAN" on it.

"Are you here with someone?"

"Thank you. And to answer your question, yes, I'm here waiting for someone."

"Well, if he or she doesn't show up, I'm right over there, sweetheart." The man pointed to a table full of men that were dressed similar to him.

"Okay, I'll keep that in mind, sir."

"Sir?" the man said quickly.

"Sweetheart, my name is Ronnie, but everyone around the way calls me Big Ron. And what's your name?" he asked, trying to give Ciara his best Denzel Washington smile.

"Catherine," Ciara replied, laughing to herself.

"You said Catherine?" the man repeated.

"Yes. Now it was nice talking to you, sir…or Big Ron, but I'm about to go and freshen up a little in the ladies' room."

"Well, alright. Don't forget I'm right over there, sweetheart."

Trust me, I won't, Ciara thought, as she almost tripped while trying to get away from the man. *This isn't working. I'm looking and smelling good, but I haven't seen anyone in here worth my time. I need to go somewhere else.*

Just when Ciara was about to walk towards the exit, a man grabbed her hand.

"Hey there, I don't mean to bother you, but do you want to dance before you leave?" He was one smooth brother.

"How did you know I was about to leave?"

"Because I saw you over there talking to your uncle, and I figured he told you to go home." the distinguished gentleman said, showing off his pearly white teeth.

"Oh, I see you got jokes," Ciara said flirtatiously, while looking the man up and down.

Moments later, she found herself dancing with the

Steven Morgan gentleman.

The smell of his cologne mixed with the natural scent of his skin was intoxicating. His appearance was mesmerizing. Ciara couldn't control herself. He was about 6'1", 200 pounds, and had light skin, with short, curly, jet-black hair and light brown eyes. He was built like a Chicago Bears football player. Ciara didn't know what was better, his Armani suit or his physique. He was the perfect person for the night.

"Last call!" the DJ announced over Fabulous' "Throw It in the Bag".

"Wow! I didn't realize it was so late," the man said, glancing at his black-face Movado watch. "Are you okay getting home tonight?"

"Yes, but I need you to tuck me in," Ciara said confidently with no shame in her game.

Without saying a word, he grabbed her hand, and they immediately left the club.

The key card couldn't open up the hotel door fast enough, because it seemed like Ciara was about to take her clothes off right there in the hallway. After they entered the room, she and the man fell onto the bed while they kissed. Ciara anxiously pulled the covers back and undressed all the way down to her purple-laced bra and g-string set. The man slowly undressed, too, but stopped when he got to his underwear.

"What's wrong?" Ciara asked, while sitting up in the bed, exposing her 36-DD breast.

"Nothing, just turn off that light so we can get this started."

That's what I'm talking about. Break me off, baby, Ciara thought as she slid off her g-string.

She reached into her purse that was on the floor, grabbed a pack of Magnum condoms from inside, and handed it to him. The room was completely dark and Ciara was ready to get sexually handled.

"Is everything okay?"

"Yeah, but this condom doesn't fit," the guy said.

"Damn, how big are you, baby?" Ciara asked, then attempted to reach for the man's dick in the dark. "You must be like thirteen inches or something."

"Don't!" he screamed.

"What's wrong with you?" Concerned by the man's reaction, she reached over and turned on the light.

"This condom is too big. I need a regular condom. Do you have a regular-size rubber?"

"Regular size? No, baby, you need that little top hat from the Monopoly game," Ciara replied, as she started to laugh.

"What? I'm just a little below average!"

"No, below average is like four or five inches. Right now, I think a doorstopper is bigger than you."

"Oh, it's like that, hoe?" The man jumped out of the bed.

"First of all, Mini Me, don't call me out of my name again!" Ciara said, pointing in the man's face.

"Fuck you, chick!" he shouted, and then started to put his clothes back on.

With the intent to harm, the man walked to the other side of the bed, reached over, and punched Ciara in the face twice. He grabbed her purse and fled from the hotel room.

"What the fuck!" Ciara screamed, as she fell back onto the bed, holding the side where she received the blows. Still dazed, she managed to grab the phone and dial 9-1-1. About twenty minutes later, the police finally showed up.

"Damn, it's about fucking time! A bitch almost died trying to wait on y'all."

The officer ignored her exaggeration as he glanced around the room. After about fifteen minutes of answering questions, Ciara was upset.

"I'm tired of answering the same damn questions!" she

Steven Morgan

yelled at the police officer, while holding an icepack to her black eye. "Go and find that bastard, because he has all of my information."

"Mrs. Blackwell, you said he didn't rape you, and we only can go by the information you gave us."

"I told you his name is John Trent. What else do you need to know? You're questioning me like I punched myself in the face. I think I'm supposed to feel like a victim."

"I thought you said his name was Justin Trent?" the officer said, looking at her suspiciously.

"Whatever, just go and find him please!"

Ciara knew she didn't know the man's name. She was so focused on accomplishing her goal that she didn't even bother to ask the man his name.

"Well, that's all the questions we have for now, Mrs. Blackwell. We will contact you if we have any information on the suspect and your property. Are you okay with a ride home tonight, ma'am?"

"Yes, I'm just fine." She threw the icepack to the floor.

The police officer nodded and left the room.

Ciara could not go home now out of fear that the unnamed attacker would be there waiting for her. Tonight, she would have to stay at the hotel room and leave first thing in the morning. Then, her next step would be going home to retrieve some of her belongings. Her mind was set on going down south to stay with her aunt until things settled down.

And here I was about to have sex with a complete stranger just so I could feel better about myself. I guess it's just time to grow up, Ciara thought, while watching the water from the icepack drip onto the carpet.

Chapter 9

"Do you think I'm fucking stupid? What the hell is going on?" Pink yelled.

"Calm down, baby. I don't think you understand." Shawn quickly closed the bedroom door.

"What is it that I don't understand? You said we were going to have a threesome, not you and another man running a fucking train on me!"

"No, he just wants to watch. He's paying us five hundred dollars just to watch us have sex. Think about it, baby. This is easy money, and we don't have to do nothing but have sex in front of him."

Shawn kissed Pink on the forehead to try and calm her down. He didn't come this far for her not to let him have his way. He was exhausting all of his options in getting her loose. The combination of Nuvo and weed had her thought process cloudy as she tried to understand what was going on.

"How do you know him?"

"It's a long story. I'll tell you after we get this money, baby."

"I guess we can make this happen, but let me get drunk first. Remember, I'm only doing this for you."

Shawn grabbed Pink's hand and guided her back into the living room where his company was waiting. Pink had a distraught look on her face as she sat down on the couch directly across from the outlandish looking man. After about an hour of drinking Nuvo and Coronas, Byron began to get

Steven Morgan

impatient.

"Can we get this party started?" Byron suggested, smacking his lips.

Shawn didn't waste any more time as he reached over and began kissing Pink, who wasn't quite drunk yet.

She just wanted to be done with this adult game of freaky charades. She had done some things in her life, but this was a little out of her league.

As Shawn kissed her, he started removing her clothes, as well as his, too. During this time, she peeked over at Byron, who was on the other end of the couch with his eyes closed, moaning as he stroked himself inside his pants. She wanted to keep a close eye on him because she didn't know him well enough to get relaxed. Shawn whispered erotic words in Pink's ear, trying to get a response from her, but she remained quiet on the couch, not interested.

"Byron, I think she's out cold and drunk. Come here."

Trying to be undetected, Pink snuck a look at Byron and noticed he was taking off his clothes.

If this man touches me, I'm going the fuck off, Pink repeated in her head over and over again as she closed her eyes again completely.

The couch began to softly rock, but she didn't feel the gentle touching that Shawn was applying to her body anymore. After slowly opening her eyes, she saw Byron on his knees in front of Shawn, swallowing all of his manhood.

"What the fuck!" she yelled.

Shawn quickly jumped back and pushed Byron's head away from his penis.

"Pink, I can explain everything." Shawn quickly tried to pull up his shorts over his erected penis, while Pink grabbed her clothes and ran towards the front door.

"Pink, stop!"

"Get away from me!" she screamed, while trying to put

her clothes back on.

"Just listen to me. Just listen, baby!"

"Baby? Something's really wrong with you, Shawn. Fuck you!" She darted towards the front door.

"Stay right here, Byron. I'll be right back."

Not panicking, Byron slowly got up and sat back on the couch like everything was normal. By the time Shawn made it outside, Pink was halfway down the block. Without a second thought, he jumped into his car to chase after her. As he backed out of the parking space, he felt a bump under his wheel, as if he ran something over.

"What the hell was that?"

Shawn jumped out of his car and saw Toby lying partially under the car.

"Oh my God! Call 9-1-1! Someone please help me!" Shawn yelled.

By the time the police and ambulance arrived at the scene, Toby was dead. His leg was mangled under the car, and he was bleeding from his mouth. Blood continued to pour from a large gash on the right side of his head as the paramedics performed different emergency procedures on him. It was a gruesome scene to say the least, but the onlookers kept a steady eye on the dead man's body. One man stood next to Toby's lifeless body reciting scriptures from his bible. A female officer escorted that man away from the scene, while three other officers handcuffed Shawn.

He was taken to the station for further questioning. At the police station, Shawn was still bothered about running Toby over. While being drilled with questions, he didn't give the detectives any eye contact.

"Now let's try this again. What happened inside of your home before you went outside and got into your car?" one of the detectives asked, as he blew smoke into Shawn's face.

"I already fucking told you! I got into an argument with

Steven Morgan

my girlfriend and that's it!"

"Are you sure you didn't hit her, because you were just recently here for beating up your other girlfriend, Kim Morton?"

"Fuck you! I told you I didn't touch her! I want my lawyer right now!"

"Get this drunken piece of shit out of my face! Tell that bullshit to the judge in the morning!"

The officers that were standing by escorted Shawn out of the interrogation room and back to the holding cell. The next morning, he was in court.

"Bail denied! The trial will be held four months from now on October fifteenth. Have a good day," the tall, slender, elderly judge yelled from his black, oversized, leather chair.

As Shawn stood up from the bench with his feet shackled and wrists handcuffed, he glanced around to see if he knew any of the faces that were staring at him in the courtroom. He knew his life wasn't his anymore once he left the packed room. He now belonged to the state. His feet were stuck in one place as the officers tried to escort him into another holding area.

"You have to wait here for a while because you're going to another location, Blackwell. We have some more people to process first. So, sit tight."

After about three hours of waiting, the van for the inmates finally arrived and transported them to their new home. The drive to the prison was quiet but not peaceful, and it got worse the closer the bus got to its destination. The cold, slate gray color of the building was an instant reminder that the next few months would be just the same.

They were transferred from the bus to the intake area of the prison, and finally to the cages. Shawn and the other inmates slowly walked in a straight line as they headed to their cells. The sound of the metal chains scraping the floor was enough to make one of the new inmates vomit. Since it was something they saw everyday on the job, the guards didn't bother to check on the ill inmate.

"Welcome to our world, bitch!" one of the guards whispered to Shawn, while shoving him into the cell.

Shawn didn't respond as he watched the cell door close behind him. The sound of the cell locking made him jittery.

"You know the routine, fool! Follow my rules or else that's your ass!" Shawn's cellmate yelled, as he continued to do his push-ups on the cold concrete floor. "Did you hear me, nigga?" the man said, getting up from the ground.

"Yeah, I heard you."

"Good. Now we have an understanding of one another. What's your name, homie?" he asked, while attempting to put on his shirt.

"Shawn, bitch!"

Swiftly, Shawn grabbed the man while his shirt was still over his head. The two fell onto the bed, as the man tried to swing at him. However, Shawn had him in an awkward position and began to ram the man's head against the bedrail.

"Motherfucker, you don't know me! I'm gonna kill you!" the man screamed, as blood from his head began to seep through his shirt.

The other inmates heard the commotion and began to cheer for Shawn's cellmate. Shawn seemed to be in a zone while he continued to fight. If he would have allowed the man to disrespect him, it would have been a problem for the next three months.

Moments later, about fifteen guards ran in and broke up the fight.

"Stop, you black bastard," the guard yelled, as he grabbed Shawn by the back of his neck and arm.

The injured man finally got back onto his feet with the blood leaking from the side of his head.

Steven Morgan

"We have a tough one on our hands here. First day and he's already in here kicking ass," a guard yelled, while pushing Shawn out of the cell. "Take his ass to the hole, and he can forget about eating for the next couple of days, too!"

The guards led him to the basement where the hole was located. It was like a jail inside of a jail. The air was thick and muggy. The walls were concrete and malicious. Nothing was good about it, except the time when the inmate was let out of the hole and back into the general population.

Shawn was still furious about the fight. "Fuck y'all! The guy came after me!"

"Don't worry about it, because you'll have plenty of time to think about what you did. Get the fuck in there, boy!"

The guard removed Shawn's handcuffs and pushed him into the soiled, dark hole. Shawn couldn't believe what was going on. He sat down on the damp concrete and made a pillow with his bloody shirt.

******

The next morning, as Ciara drove to her house, she tried to put together in her head all of the events that had taken place recently in her life.

"I need to go to church," Ciara said, as she glanced over at the small cross that hung from her review mirror.

While pulling up in front of her house, she didn't notice anything out of the ordinary. After looking around to see if any windows were broken, she felt safe enough to venture inside. She carefully opened the front door and was shocked at the scene before her. The house looked like a tornado had ripped through it. All of the furniture was flipped over, cabinets were open, and her flat screen TV was gone out of the living room.

"Damn! I have to grab what I can and leave."

Ciara raced up the stairs to her bedroom. As she rushed

in and out of her closets and bathroom, her cell phone began to ring, displaying a number she didn't recognize.

"Yes, who is this?"

"Hello, this is Decorey. How have you been, Ciara?"

"I'm okay. Just in the process of moving right now, that's all."

"Oh, I'm so sorry to bother you."

"No, it's okay, but can I call you back later?"

"Of course, you can. By the way, did you need any help moving? I have a truck if you need it."

"Yeah, but I don't want to trouble you, Decorey."

"Trouble me? It'll be my pleasure."

So she gave him the address and waited for him to arrive. He made it to her house in about twenty minutes with the moving truck, and before she knew it, the truck was packed and ready to go.

"I really appreciate the help, Decorey. How much do I owe you?"

"How about dinner and maybe a movie?" he answered, while pulling down the back door on the moving truck.

"Well, I was planning on going out of town for a while, but I guess I can wait until after our date."

"No, I don't want to hold up your plans."

"It's okay. I need to clear my mind anyway, and you might help me do so."

He wiped a bead of sweat off of his forehead and smiled. "Good. Now where are we going with your stuff?"

"I'm going to put everything into a storage unit until I get back from out of town."

"Lead the way," he said, as he climbed into the truck.

After about two hours of hauling furniture, they had everything piled into the storage unit and were now standing back in front of her house.

"So what time do you want to go out?"

Steven Morgan

Before he could answer, his cell phone rang. He looked at the screen and Pink's name was on the display.

"Excuse me for a minute. I really need to take this call."

Decorey walked a few feet away so he could answer Pink's call.

"Hey, I really need to talk to you. Shawn cheated on me and he's in jail and I don't know what to do," she rambled on.

"Okay, calm down first. I'll call you right back in about five minutes."

After ending the call, he looked back at Ciara to see if she had heard his conversation.

"Hey Ciara, I really have to go and take care of some business…" Before he could finish his sentence, his phone rang again. "I'm sorry once again, but let me take this call."

Damn, he has a hot line going on, Ciara thought.

"Yeah, I already heard about it. I'll talk to you about it later." He closed his cell phone, ending his call. "Sorry about that, Ciara, but we can go out around seven o'clock, if that's okay with you."

"Yeah, that's a good time."

"Cool. I'll see you then," he said, then jumped into the moving truck and pulled off. As soon as he was down the street, he called Pink back.

"Hey, I had the worse night of my life," Pink's voice crackled.

"What happened?" Decorey asked, while turning up the volume on his cell phone.

"I found out that Shawn's gay! He told me that this man was going to pay us five hundred dollars to watch us have sex. I didn't want to do it, but I knew we needed the money. So, I played like I was drunk and they started to take all of my clothes off of me. But, when I opened my eyes, the man was giving Shawn a blowjob. I got up and ran out the door and down the street. When I returned home, my neighbor told me that Shawn ran over a homeless man while he was backing out of the parking lot trying to chase after me."

"So where are you at now?"

"I'm leaving and I'm never coming back. I'm on the Greyhound. I just can't take it anymore. I'm never coming back to Chicago again."

"Wait! When will I get to see you again? I only met you once and we just talked over the phone."

"I know, Decorey. You've been like a big brother to me since day one. Thank you for being there for me, but I must get away from everyone and everything in Chicago. I have to go," Pink said, and then ended the call with Decorey without even saying goodbye.

He dialed her number again, but his call was sent straight to her voicemail.

Goodbye, Pink, Decorey thought, as he placed his cell phone on the passenger seat.

Chapter 10

Ciara didn't have anything to wear on a date, so she decided to stop by the mall. In the parking lot, she noticed a car that was similar to Kim's. Ciara wished the car did belong to Kim, but she never thought she would be so lucky.

Just as she was about to get out of the car, though, she spotted Kim walking out of the mall with a bag in her hand. As soon as Kim noticed Ciara, she tried to run to her car, but Ciara met her there just as she was getting in.

"Slow down, bitch!" Ciara reached in and grabbed Kim by her hair.

"Please stop!"

"The only way I'm stopping is if my heart stops beating!"

Kim was able to reach into her purse and grab a small canister of mace.

"You bitch!" Ciara screamed, trying to cover her face from the strong pepper spray.

Kim continued to spray the mace in her face until the can was empty. Ciara fell to the ground rubbing her eyes and screaming to the top of her lungs. Kim quickly jumped out of the car and repeatedly kicked her in the stomach. A couple of people gathered around, but no one made an attempt to get involved. With Ciara lying on the ground coughing and grimacing from the mace, Kim tried to yell, but her speech was still slurred from the hotel beating.

"Fuck you and your momma, bitch!"

Kim then jumped back into her car and sped away, leaving Ciara and their friendship behind. A concerned bystander thought it was safe to get closer and offer her assistance once Kim took off.

"Do you want us to call the police, miss?"

"Go fuck yourself! I'm okay!"

Ciara was agitated about the whole situation. With her eyes puffy and red, she went inside the mall. From the way everyone was staring at her, someone would have thought she was a celebrity. About twenty minutes later, she was able to see clearly.

Again, another stranger asked, "Are you okay? Would you like for us to call the paramedics?"

"I'm okay. Why you ask?"

"Because it looks like you need medical attention."

"Excuse you," Ciara replied.

"I didn't mean to upset you, ma'am. I was just trying to help."

"How about you help me by getting out of my face, bitch?"

The woman knew Ciara was ready for whatever at this point, so she just politely walked away.

"That hoe got some nerve," Ciara said, as she walked into the clothing store.

It didn't take her long to find something to wear for her date with Decorey.

"Damn, look at my face. I'm going to fuck Kim up when I see her again."

******

Feeling horrible about what went down with Ciara, Kim tried to hide her pain with food. She swallowed a fork full of Chinese rice. They were as close as sisters for most of their lives, but in such a short period of time, the two had become strangers. Kim knew she was wrong for messing with Shawn, but she wanted Ciara to forgive her because there was no way she would be able to live with them being enemies. Kim looked over at her cell phone that was lying on the bed next to her. It was time for her to try again.

Ciara couldn't believe her eyes when she saw Kim's name displayed on her cell phone. She picked up the phone and gave Kim a tongue-lashing.

"Bitch, you got some nerve calling me like everything is cool."

"Ciara, I want to meet you somewhere so we can talk about everything."

"I can't understand your retarded ass. You're gonna have to speak English, hoe."

"Please, Ciara, can we talk about this?"

"There really isn't anything you can say. You played me. You fucked my man, bitch! What is there to be said?"

"I have something that's troubling me, and you're the only person that I can confide in. My soul is hurting, and I can't fight it by myself."

Although Kim's speech was impaired, Ciara could hear and feel the pain that Kim was expressing to her.

"Okay, you pick the spot."

"Can we meet by the police station on Madison?"

"Why do you want to meet by the police station? Are you trying to set me up?"

"No, I just don't want to get into another altercation with

you. I'm not going to take up too much of your time. I just want to clear things up between us."

"Fine, meet me there in thirty minutes," Ciara said, then hung up.

God, please keep me from beating her ass when I see her. I feel like I'm losing my mind. Shawn and Kim are going to have me in the fucking nuthouse, Ciara thought, as she drove to the meeting location.

When she arrived, she saw Kim and decided to get out of the car first. Ciara hoped God remembered what she just asked him as she walked over to her.

"Okay, start talking," Ciara said once she was standing in front of her.

"I'm sorry for anything I have ever done to hurt you and our friendship, Ciara. I never meant for any of this to happen between us."

"Kim, I just want to know why? Why me? Why my man?" Ciara asked, while reaching for her cell phone that was vibrating in her pocket.

"Please don't," Kim begged.

"Please don't what?"

"I thought you was about to pull out something."

"When did you become so damn scared?"

"The night you put that beatdown on me," she replied.

Both women caught a glimpse of their old friendship and laughed.

"Ciara, listen, Shawn isn't any good for you. I know it takes two to tango, but Shawn forced himself on me."

"But how did you get into that situation where he could force himself on you?"

"I don't know. I really don't know. I was stupid, jealous, and drunk. You've always talked about how good Shawn was to you, and I wanted to experience it for myself."

"Experience what?"

"Happiness! I'm sorry, and if you hate me, I understand." Kim wiped a tear from her cheek.

"I don't hate you. I just wish you would have used better judgment for this one. Shawn is my husband, and you're my best friend."

"I know, and I hope that one day you'll forgive me for everything I've done to you."

"Kim, you know I'll forgive you, but I'll never forget what you did to me. I know how Shawn is. He's been cheating on me since day one. I didn't want to be alone again. I didn't want to end up like my mother. Her life ended the day my father left. I didn't want to die alone and sad. This is something we will have to just somehow erase if we want to remain friends."

Kim's face lit up. "So, you forgive me?" she asked, then looked down at the ground.

"Yes, I forgive you. Other than God, you're all I have." Ciara reached over and hugged Kim. "I'm sorry for what I did to you. I just lost control."

"The past is now the past, Ciara. Let's just move on and rebuild our friendship."

"I've been through a lot lately. My life is out of control, and I'm in need of a vacation. Do you want to go downtown and have a drink?"

"Sure. I don't have anything to do. Let's go," Kim replied.

As soon as they arrived at the restaurant, they spotted a girl from the neighborhood.

"Hey, isn't that Tania, Kim?"

"Yeah, I think so, but damn, she got big as hell since high school."

"Hey girl!" Ciara quickly waved at Tania, who was walking

towards their table.

"I haven't seen y'all since high school. How are you?"

"We're doing just fine. How about you, Tania?" Ciara asked.

"I'm doing okay, just getting bigger and bigger as you can see," Tania replied, while taking a seat.

"No, I didn't even notice," Kim said, looking at Ciara.

"Well, anyway, y'all heard what happened to crackhead Toby, right?"

Some shit never changes. This hoe still has her ear to everything that goes on in Chicago, Ciara thought.

"Toby is dead, girl! A car hit him the other day. They said his legs were broken and half of his head was smashed in."

"Are you serious?" Ciara asked.

"Yes girl, and guess who they took to jail for hitting him? Shawn Blackwell!"

"Shawn!" Ciara screamed, as she stood up from the table, knocking over a glass of fresh lemon water in the process.

"Yeah. From what I hear, Toby was going over there to fight Shawn or something like that."

"Wait, I'm not understanding you, Tania. Why would Toby want to fight Shawn?" Ciara asked.

Kim knew what was going on between Shawn and Toby, but remained silent.

"Well, my brother hangs with Toby and those other dopefiends on the block, and he said Toby thought Shawn wanted to kill him for some strange reason. And yes, my brother is strung out, too. So, don't look at me like that, Kim."

"Oh my God! I have to find out what's going on. I can't believe this. When it rains, it pours." Ciara placed her hands on her forehead.

"Well, I've said enough already. Let me go. It was nice seeing y'all again." Tania grabbed three packs of sugar, then forced her body from between the chair and table to get up. "I wouldn't pay for lemonade if I were you, girl. You better make your own like I do."

After Tania walked off, Kim got up and sat on the other side of the table to console Ciara.

"It's like ever since me and Shawn broke up, everything has gone downhill for me."

Kim knew the real reason why Shawn and Toby had beef with one another, but if she told Ciara, it would just break her heart even more.

"Come on, Ciara, let's get out of here. You're more than welcome to come back to my place."

"No, I don't want to be a burden on you," Ciara said, while grabbing her purse and standing. "Besides, I think I need some time to myself."

"Are you sure?"

"No, I'm not sure. I just don't know what else to do."

"Come on, I'll drive. We can just leave your car here until we find out what's going on with Shawn."

Chapter 11

"Have you ever tried this before?" the tattooed inmate calmly asked.

"I don't smoke that shit," Shawn said, as he continued to shave in the foggy bathroom mirror. "What is that anyway, because it has a funny smell to it?"

"Man, this ain't nothing but some homemade crack. Some people call it crank. The crew that runs the 2nd deck sells this shit for eighty-five dollars a gram."

"Crank? Yeah, you can keep that for yourself. I don't fuck with none of that stupid shit."

"What's the deal with you? I've never seen you in here before." Shawn really didn't want to have a conversation with the inmate, but he couldn't afford to have another fight when he still had some months to go before his court date. He sighed before answering.

"That's because I was in the hole for my first couple of weeks. I got into a fight with this funny-looking dude," Shawn replied, then splashed some warm water on his face.

"You're a man of very little words, I see," the inmate said, while checking out his reflection in the mirror next to Shawn.

"Yeah, and I plan on keeping it that way, homie."

"Damn, playboy, I'm not your enemy, and I didn't put you in this motherfucker either! So, you can save that tough guy act for

somebody who gives a fuck! Understand, nigga?"
The inmate looked Shawn up and down before walking away.
"Finish up, punk!" the husky guard yelled.
"I'm done here," Shawn replied, as he placed his towel on his shoulder.
While being escorted back down the hall, Shawn noticed the man that he had gotten into the fight with sitting in a nearby cell. The man didn't say a word. He just stared at Shawn the entire time. The guard yelled for Shawn's cell to be opened. Inside, a tall, slender white guy with sandy brown hair was stretched across the bottom bunk.
"Turn around!" the guard yelled, then roughly removed Shawn's handcuffs.
"So what's the deal with you?" the white man asked Shawn, as he yawned and sat up in his bunk.
"I'm Shawn, and you?"
"I'm Paul, but everybody calls me Scissors," the man said, offering to shake Shawn's hand.
"Scissors?" Shawn repeated. "Why does everyone call you Scissors?"
"About two months ago, I stabbed two guards with some scissors I made out of the wire from my bunk."
Shawn slowly swallowed.
"But you're cool, Black Man Shawn. I just hate these bitch-ass guards in here!" Paul yelled, while looking out of the cell hoping to catch the attention of the guards that were nearby.
"So do you want me to call you Scissors or Paul?"
"I don't give a shit what you call me, Black Man Shawn."
"Why do you keep calling me Black Man Shawn? Are you a white supremacist or something?"
"Because all of the Shawn's that I know in here are white. So what are you in for, Black Man Shawn?"

"I accidentally killed a pedestrian," Shawn regretfully replied.
"Damn, you're the second person I've met today that's in here for manslaughter."
"Manslaughter? No, I'm just waiting on my next court date. My bail was denied when I went to court the first time."
"Well, Black Man Shawn, you need a good lawyer and a prayer."
"Whatever! I'm innocent, and my lawyer is going to prove it."
"Were you drunk or something when this happened?"
"It doesn't matter, because I'm going to beat the case."
"Well, I'll let you think that, Black Man Shawn. Do you want to play some two-hand Spades?"
"Yeah, but can you stop calling me Black Man Shawn?"

******

Day after day, Shawn tried to occupy his time in jail by doing something constructive. Five days out of the week Shawn exercised and played cards with Paul and other inmates. The other two days of the week Shawn spent praying and trying to contact Pink and Byron. He was unclear about what was going on outside of jail, because he didn't have contact with anyone. He couldn't even locate Eric. He tried to contact Ciara, but he wasn't able to reach her either. It felt like he didn't even exist to anyone anymore.

Seconds seemed like days, and days seemed like years to him. All he had was a deck of cards and his weird-ass cellmate.

"Hey, Black Man Shawn, what did you do before you got yourself locked up?"
"Well, it's a long story, and I really don't want to go into details."

Steven Morgan

"Go into details? I just wanted to know if you had a family or worked. Trust me, I don't want to know or hear your life story."
"Well, I was in a strange situation. I lived a complicated life. I had a wife at home and a mistress on the side. And to make a long story short, I don't have either of them right now."
"Damn, I'm sorry to hear that, Black Man Shawn," Paul said, clearing his throat.
"It's cool, because I knew what I was doing. I thought that I could have my cake and eat it, too, if you know what I mean."
"So who is Byron?" Paul asked.
"How in the hell do you know about Byron?" Shawn said, jumping up from his bunk.
"I don't know who Byron is, but you're always saying his name in your sleep. I have to ask you this. Do you play on both sides of the fence?"
"Both sides of the fence? What the hell are you talking about? Don't you ever ask me some stupid shit like that again!"
Paul didn't respond because he knew Shawn was lying about his involvement with Byron.
"I can't believe you would ask me something like that!" Shawn yelled, as he climbed up to the top bunk.
Shawn couldn't deny his involvement with Byron to himself. He thought about him more than he did anyone else. He wasn't sure why Byron was on his mind so much. Maybe he felt Byron was the reason for him being in his current situation.
The next day, Shawn met with his lawyer to work out the details of his case. He also wanted his lawyer to contact Ciara since he hadn't heard from her since their night at the Seneca Hotel.
"Hey Tim, can you please do me a favor and try to get in contact with my wife?"
"Well, I've tried several times, but Mrs. Blackwell isn't living at that address anymore. The number you gave me is going

straight to voicemail, as well."
Shawn didn't give it a second thought.
"Well, I'll worry about her later." Shawn shrugged it off. "For
now, please try to do something to get me out of here sooner.
I'm about to go crazy in here. All I see is people fighting,
people getting raped, and every five minutes somebody is
passing a kite to me to give to another nigga. I need to get out of
here real fast."
"I'm trying my best. Just give me some more time."
"Well, you need to try harder! I thought you were on my side? I
thought this wouldn't drag on like this? Those were your words,
not mines!" He became agitated.
"Shawn, wait!"
"Fuck you. Just do your damn job. Do your fucking job!"
After visitation, Shawn went back to his cell for a quick shower.
The walk from the visiting room to the cell didn't last too long.
As Shawn walked down the dark and murky hallway, he could
hear the screams of another inmate being taken advantage of.
Every second of the day he prayed that he would not be the next
victim.
Upon returning to his cell, he spotted Paul rambling through his
belongings. "What the hell are you doing in my shit?"
"Relax, Black Man Shawn. I was just borrowing some things."
"Calm down, ladies. There's plenty of room down in the hole
you know," the guard said, while tapping the bars with his club.
"You can't borrow shit of mines." Shawn tried to snatch his roll
of toilet tissue that Paul had in his hand, but he didn't succeed.
"What the hell is wrong with you?" Paul asked in an angry
voice.
"Fuck you!"
Shawn threw a punch at Paul, who quickly moved out of the
way. As a result, Shawn's fist hit the top bed rail instead of

connecting to Paul's face. Paul grabbed Shawn and pulled his arms behind his back.

"Let me go, you fucking freak!" Shawn yelled, as he tried to break free.

However, Paul quickly grabbed the bottom sheet from his bed and began to tie Shawn's hands up. Shawn struggled to free himself, but couldn't pull away. Although Paul was tall and slim, he had natural strength from the three hundred push-ups he did every day.

"You black motherfucker!" Paul screamed, then hit Shawn in the back of his head. "I know you like this. Is this what you use to do to Byron, you black pussy?"

Paul reached into his sock and pulled out a small pair of scissors. When he tried to put his hand over Shawn's mouth, Shawn bit him.

"You black bastard! I got a surprise for you, motherfucker!" Paul began to stab Shawn in the lower part of his back with the scissors.

"Help me!" Shawn screamed in a shuddering voice.

Paul took another poke into Shawn's back. He then quickly began to pull down his pants with one hand, while holding Shawn with the other one. Shawn was weak and couldn't defend himself. Blood was everywhere. While removing Shawn's pants, Paul could hear the guards running down the hall towards their cell. Just as Paul began to penetrate him, the guards came in and tackled him to the floor. Meanwhile, Shawn was lying unconscious in a pool of blood.

"Someone go and get help. This guy needs help immediately!"

******

The next day, Kim was at Ciara's house trying to grab the

rest of her things, when Shawn's lawyer came by. Kim noticed a black Lexus pulling up in front of Ciara's door.

"How are you doing, Ciara?" Shawn's lawyer said, as he exited his clean two-door Lexus coupe.

"Hi, but I'm not Ciara. She's at my house resting up."

"Well, are you her sister or just a friend of the family?"

"Yes, I'm her sister, and who are you?" Kim asked in an impudent way.

"I'm Shawn's lawyer, and I really need to get in contact with Ciara because Shawn was hurt in a fight yesterday at the jail."

"What! Are you serious?" Kim squealed. Dazed, she dropped everything she had in her hands.

"He's in the intensive care unit down at Stroger's Hospital, and he's in grave condition."

"Oh my God! What happened?"

"Well, I didn't get the full story yet, but I do know that he was stabbed about six times. I just need you to contact his wife for me and let her know what's going on."

"Okay, I'll be sure to do that. Thank you so much." Kim quickly grabbed her cell phone from out of her purse and called Ciara. *Please pick up the damn phone. Please, Ciara!*
Ciara could hear Kim crying on the other end as soon as she answered.

"What's wrong, Kim?"

"I just talked to Shawn's lawyer, and he said Shawn was stabbed six times yesterday. He's in the intensive care unit at Stroger's Hospital!"

"Oh no! What happened to my…?" She began to wail uncontrollably before she could even get the word husband out of her mouth.

"I don't know, but his lawyer just came over here and told me to contact you. I'm on my way back to the house to take you up

there.”
“I don’t have time. I’m going to catch a cab to my car, and then I’m going to the hospital.”
“Okay, Ciara, I’ll meet you there.”
On the way to the hospital, Ciara prayed at least ten times for God to spare Shawn’s life. She couldn’t foresee living without him. She felt like her life was spinning out of control. Everything that could go wrong went wrong.
When Ciara finally made it to the hospital, she parked in a nearby handicap spot, without hesitation. She didn’t even bother to lock her doors after jumping out of the car.
“Can I help the next person?” the man yelled from behind the counter, as Ciara walked through the double doors.
“Yes, I’m here to see my husband, Shawn Blackwell. He’s in the intensive care unit!”
“Just a moment,” the frail man said, then got up and slowly walked to the back office.
About five minutes later, the frail employee and another well-dressed man emerged from the back.
“Mrs. Blackwell, could you please come with us?” the man said, as he held open the swinging door.
“What’s the matter? Is Shawn okay?”
He and Ciara walked into the back office of the emergency room.
“Have a seat,” the man insisted.
“No! Is Shawn okay? Tell me something about my husband!” Ciara yelled, becoming hysterical.
“I’m sorry to inform you of this, Mrs. Blackwell, but your husband died about twenty minutes ago during surgery.”
The man tried to place his hand on Ciara’s shoulder, but she pulled away from him.
“Died? No, you’re fucking lying! Where’s my fucking

husband? I want to see my husband right fucking now!”
Ciara was so loud that the other people outside could hear her.
“No, no, no, this can’t be happening!” Ciara cried, as she fell to
her knees. “I want to see him! Please just let me see my
husband!” Ciara reached for the man’s pants leg.
“I’m so sorry, Mrs. Blackwell.” The man helped Ciara off of the
floor and sat her down on a chair. “Hey Scott, grab me some
tissue and a cup of water. Is there anything I can do to help you,
Mrs. Blackwell?”
“Dead? This can’t be happening. Please tell me this isn’t so!
What happened? How did this happen?” Ciara cried.
“Mr. Blackwell was severely stabbed yesterday during an
altercation with another inmate.”
“Stabbed? Why did someone stab him? He wouldn’t hurt a
soul.”
“I’m not sure, Mrs. Blackwell. There weren’t any witnesses,
and the inmate who got into the dispute with Mr. Blackwell
isn’t talking to us about what actually happened in the cell.”
He could see the pain and agony in Ciara’s face. Unfortunately,
he had seen the anguish on many faces over the years of
working in an emergency room. It was all too much of a
familiar scene.
“I know this is painful for you, but I need you or a family
member of Mr. Blackwell’s to view the body.”
“No, I can’t do it! I just can’t do it!” Ciara couldn’t take the
reality of seeing Shawn lying dead on a table.
“But someone has to view the body.”
Ciara jumped up and ran out of the room. “God help me!” she
yelled, as she searched through her purse for her cell phone to
call Kim.
Kim didn’t answer the back-to-back calls from her, and she
didn’t know which way to turn. Part of her life was now over.

Steven Morgan

Her other half was missing from the puzzle. Shawn's death left an empty void inside of Ciara. She couldn't stand the sight of the hospital anymore and had to leave.

After leaving the hospital, she decided to take the back road to cut around the rush-hour traffic. Flashing ambulance lights and road flares were in the intersection where Ciara was trying to turn. Traffic was at a halt, so Ciara tried to call Kim again. As the tow truck ahead of Ciara and other vehicles moved, she saw Kim's car smashed against the wall on the opposite side of the road. Ciara jumped out of her car and ran towards the scene.

"Miss, stop!" the officer yelled, grabbing her.

"That's my friend in that car!" Ciara yelled to the top of her lungs.

Kim was slumped over in the car with her head on the steering wheel.

"Kim! Oh my goodness!" Ciara cried when she saw the stream of blood coming from her forehead.

"We have to hurry up!" a firefighter yelled to his crew.

The three men finally pulled Kim from the car just as it caught on fire. Her body was flimsy and bloody, and it looked like the left side of her face was smashed in from the impact of her head hitting the steering wheel. Even worse, she wasn't showing any signs of life. The paramedics tried to revive her several times at the scene, but it was too late; DOA.

"Kim!" Ciara screamed, as they pulled the thin white sheet over her best friend's lifeless body.

Ciara started to run towards Kim, but she got nauseous and everything went black just as she fainted to the ground.

Chapter 12

About two years went by, and Ciara was still dealing with the heartrending loss of Shawn and Kim. The two closest people in Ciara's life died on the same day. When Shawn and Kim died, a part of Ciara died, as well. The love in her heart was gone. The only thing embedded inside of her soul was hate and revenge. Ciara's life had turned upside down. She wasn't the same "Ciara" that use to have all of the hustlers and old men ready to give up their life savings for her. Things didn't change much physically, but her state of mind allowed her to look like your average neighborhood dope fiend. Her hair was matted and severely damaged. Just a basic wash and set wasn't enough for Ciara's horrendous head. She needed hours of treatment to get her hair back on track and healthy. She didn't even dress the same. Her clothes were either too big for her or six years out of date. She went from Ed Hardy outfits to thrift store "everything must go" outfits. Besides the bogus attire, Ciara lost everything she had. The savings that she and Shawn had accumulated was used for Kim and Shawn's funeral. With no other source of income, Ciara eventually lost her apartment and car.

On the day her car got repossessed, Ciara walked twenty-two blocks to the car lot, just so they could tell her that she wasn't getting her car back without the $780 payment that was overdue. Not to mention the $200 in repossession fees.

On her way back from the car lot, she came home to neighbors and other people she didn't even know picking through her possessions that the sheriffs had placed outside just before she made it back. She didn't even bother to stop the raiders. She just grabbed her pictures of Shawn and Kim, and continued to walk down the street towards the bus station. Ciara wanted to leave, but she didn't even have enough money to get to the Greyhound station, let alone purchase a ticket. Her plan was to move to Macon, Georgia, and get her life back in order, but she was afraid her aunt wouldn't accept her because she hadn't spoken to her since Shawn's funeral.

Ciara walked into the phone booth counting the loose change in her hand. Ever since Shawn and Kim died, Ciara had started every day off with a prayer to God, hoping it would help her make it through the day that she was about to face. But, one particular prayer was a little different than the others:

God, please help me with any decisions I make in my life. I feel that I have no one to turn to. I don't want to feel this empty and lonely feeling anymore. Please have mercy on me for my sins. I'm a sinner, but I'm not Satan. I feel as if the world owes me something, and I'm at the point of no return. You will never put me through anything I can't handle, right? Well, why can't I handle what you've put me through thus far?

Ciara took a deep breath and dialed her aunt's phone number. The phone only rang once before her aunt answered with music blasting in the background.

"Hello! Who is this interrupting my church music?" Ciara's aunt screamed through the receiver.

"Can you hear me, Aunt Liz? It's Ciara."

"I told you motherfuckers to stop calling here! I'm not buying any of your cheap mascara!"

Click! Aunt Liz hung up the phone.

Aunt Liz was a hot mess. She listened to church music, prayed to the Lord, and cursed people out all in the same instance. Ciara patted her front pockets and realized she was out of change. She couldn't call Aunt Liz back today. Ciara was pissed off about not being able to ask her aunt if she could live with her in Georgia.

Ciara walked down the street without a purpose. Her stomach growled, so she grabbed a smashed up piece of gum out of her pocket as she walked into a nearby clothing store. She wasn't in the store for ten seconds before the clerk started watching her every move.

"I just walked into the damn store! It's four other people in here, if you haven't noticed. Why are your eyes on me?"

"Because they're my eyes," the young clerk replied, as she glanced down at Ciara's shoes and snickered.

"Oh yeah, bitch?" Ciara graciously walked over to the girl and punched her in the eye.

"Call the police, Samantha!" the clerk yelled, while lying on top of the well-dressed mannequin that broke her fall and holding her throbbing eye.

Ciara didn't run. Instead, she continued to look at the clothes until the police arrived.

"What seems to be the problem here?" the officer asked, as he removed his hat.

"I want to press everything on that hooligan over there," the girl said, now holding an icepack on her eye. "She was stealing from our establishment!"

"How does she know I was stealing something and her eye is swollen like that?" Ciara jokingly said to the officer.

The whole thing was funny to Ciara. She knew it was a possibility that she could've went to jail, but at that point, it really didn't matter to her at all.

"You can just take me to jail, officer. I really don't give a shit!" The officers did as instructed and placed Ciara under arrest. She was taken down to the station, where she would remain until she went to court the next morning to face the judge.

"Mrs. Blackwell, why did you strike the store clerk?" That was the first question the judge asked her.

"Your Honor…Judge…or whatever you want to be called…I

Steven Morgan

didn't hit her. My hand slipped and landed on her eye."

There was some chatter heard throughout the courtroom
because the people had to refrain themselves from laughing.

"Order in my courtroom! Real funny, Mrs. Blackwell. Well, in
that case, how about you slip back into your cell for another
twenty days!"

"What? I was just playing, Judge. You didn't let me finish
telling you what happened!"

The entire courtroom erupted in laughter.

"Get her out of my face!" the judge screamed.

Ciara ended up only doing thirteen days before being released a
week early for good behavior. The next day after she had been
released, Decorey spotted her walking down Madison Avenue
in a bright red sweat suit.

"Say it ain't so," Decorey said out loud after he noticed her
crossing the street.

"What is it?" Byron asked, while sharing a coffee with Decorey
at the table.

"It's Ciara Blackwell. I haven't seen her in a couple of years."

"Shawn's wife Ciara?" Byron asked in a brazen way.

Yes, and she looks like a damn mess, Decorey thought, getting
up from the table.

"Ciara!" Decorey yelled, as he held open the door and signaled
for her. "Come here!"

"Not him. Not now," Ciara mumbled, recognizing Decorey.

"Hey, how have you been?"

"I'm okay. How about yourself, Decorey?"

"I'm hanging in there. Just trying to take it one day at a time."

He could see the pain and suffering that she was going through.

"Ciara, I'm sorry to hear about what happened to your husband
and Kim. I know you had to deal with some difficult things in
your life, and I just wanted you to know that I'm here to help
you if you need me."

Ciara looked at Decorey, wondering how he knew about what

happened to Shawn and Kim. She couldn't hold back her tears
and began to cry. Decorey took her into his arms in a strong
embrace.

"Excuse me! Don't act like I'm not standing here, Decorey!"
Decorey and Ciara's moment was over.

"Byron, this is Ciara, and Ciara, this is Byron."
Ciara reached out to shake his hand.

"Anyway," Byron said, not acknowledging her handshake at all,
"what is taking you so long? Just give that thing some money so
we can finish our breakfast."

"I'm talking to an old friend of mines. Could you just give me
some more time?"

"And what does that have to do with me?"

Decorey ignored Byron's remark. "I'm sorry about that, Ciara.
I'm not going to hold you up. Do you have a number so I can
keep in touch with you?"

"No, because at the time, I'm homeless," Ciara shamefully
replied.

"Homeless? I have plenty of room for you at my place."
Byron couldn't believe what Decorey just said.

"Oh no, we don't have any room at our house, Decorey!"
 I know him from somewhere. I just can't figure out where I've
seen him before, Ciara thought to herself.

"I don't want to be a burden on you, Decorey, so I'll pass.
Thanks anyway."

"No, it'll be my pleasure. I want to help you out."

Ciara had two options at the moment. She could be stubborn
and stay out on the streets, or she had the chance of getting help
so she could get back on her feet. Ciara chose the latter. This
was her best, if not only, opportunity to get back on track.

"Okay," Ciara answered, as she lowered her head.

"Good. Now let's get out of here."

As Decorey began to walk away, Byron stepped in front of
Ciara.

Steven Morgan

"Don't think for one minute we're asking you to move in for good! My brother is just a little gullible."

Ciara hoped this punk didn't jump in her face again, because she would have no problem putting him in his place.

"Okay, Byron, I totally understand the arrangement. I'm not going to be a problem at all," she assured him.

"Thought so," he replied, while rolling his eyes and getting into the car.

******

Decorey and Byron had a three-bedroom brick house on the north side of Chicago around the Rogers Park area, which was predominantly populated with blacks and Hispanics. This was the area Decorey decided to live in when he sold his construction business last year. It was just a temporary residence for him because he was in the process of having a house built in Plainfield, a far western suburb of Chicago. Also, it wasn't too far from Byron's salon.

"When was the last time you went to the Magnificent Mile, Ciara?" Decorey asked, as he lowered the radio's volume.

"I don't even know what the Magnificent Mile is."

"What? You need to get out more. You don't know what the Magnificent Mile is and you live in Chicago?" Decorey teased.

"Please, you need to ask her when the last time soap and water touched her ass."

"Don't be rude, Byron," Decorey said, looking over at Byron in the passenger seat.

"I'm telling the truth. I've been smelling this terrible stench ever since we got in the car with her."

"Byron!" Decorey yelled, implying that he was going too far with his impolite comments.

"Whatever! I'm going to say what I feel. And I feel that she needs to wash her ass."

"Out of respect for Decorey, I'm going to remain calm, but I don't think I can continue to brush off your comments, Byron." Byron turned around in the passenger seat to face Ciara, who was sitting directly behind Decorey.

"Do you think I give a damn about how you feel, tramp? You're Decorey's little friend, not mine. So, don't get it twisted!"

"Enough, Byron! She's going to be staying with us, and that's it! This is my decision, not yours."

Byron cut his eyes at Ciara.

This little nasty-ass bitch makes me sick, Byron thought, as he turned around and pulled out some clear fingernail polish from his pouch.

As Decorey slowly turned the car down a narrow block, Ciara stared at the colorful autumn leaves that covered the street and front yards of the houses. The serene and vivid view gave her a warm feeling inside.

I really miss Shawn, she thought, while watching a young couple carry in groceries together.

Decorey parked in front of a large two-story brick home that sat on the corner of the block. Ciara got out of the car and looked around as if she had never seen a Chicago neighborhood before.

"Ciara, I'm going to get dinner started and then I'll show you around the house."

"Okay, Decorey. Where's your bathroom?"

"It's right down that hallway, on your left-hand side."

"Wait a minute," Byron said, stopping Ciara in her tracks and handing her a can of lemon-scented Lysol. "And make sure you spray everywhere."

The old Ciara would've been slapped the taste out of his mouth, but the new Ciara just wanted a decent place to lay her head while she got her plan together. She knew she had to make something happen soon, because Byron was going to make her lose her cool.

Steven Morgan

******

About two months went by, and Ciara didn't have any luck with finding a job. The fact of the matter was she never planned on looking for a job. She just needed enough time to come up with a plan to make some fast money. She knew the only way she could come up with a lump sum of cash was if she robbed some of the drug dealers from the neighborhood. It was a legit plan, but she couldn't make her move until everything was in order. Nevertheless, Ciara studied each drug corner and its daily operations. Day after day, she watched how the local drug dealers made their transactions in the neighborhood. She learned the game from a far, but she saw a lot. There were still some missing details about what was going on, but she had down the routine on drop-offs and pick-ups. She figured out the whole set-up of who did what and when they did it. Who was in charge and who were just foot soldiers. Ciara's plan was to make as much money as she could from the hustlers and then leave for Georgia before she got too hot.

The first thing Ciara needed to make the robberies happen was a gun. She took three buses to the Albany Park neighborhood to meet up with a goon named Big Geo.

"I don't have all day, Ciara. Which one do you want?"

Ciara carefully examined each gun that Geo had lying on the table in front of her.

"How much is it for this one?"

Geo looked down at Ciara's ass protruding out of her jeans. "A little of this, maybe a little of that," Geo replied, while undressing Ciara with his eyes."

"How much is it, Geo?" Ciara asked, as she admired the all-black Desert Eagle.

"That's called a Jericho 941. It's a baby Desert Eagle. Just give me four hundred."

"Four hundred? How about two-fifty and some of this Kush?"
Ciara pulled out a half ounce of purple weed.
"Damn, that shit is funky right there. I want some of that. Drop
that weed and that two-fifty," he demanded.
Ciara counted out two hundred and fifty dollars and handed it
over to Geo. He grabbed a white cloth that was near the other
guns and began to wipe his fingerprints off. The only thing she
had to do now was find herself a victim that was slipping. She
was already a step ahead of things. She had been saving all of
the money that Decorey gave her to look for a job with to buy
the gun from Big Geo.
"This motherfucker didn't come from me if you get caught,
little mama. You feel me?" he said with a stern look.
"Don't worry about that. I may be a lady, but I know the rules
of the street game. This is going to be put to good use," Ciara
said, as she wrapped the gun in between two towels and threw it
into the laundry bag she had.
She walked out of the house, got onto the CTA bus, and headed
to the storage unit on the north side that she had rented earlier
that day. When she made it there, she placed the laundry bag
inside of her assigned unit and left.

Ciara knew money was her only motivation, and she needed
bundles of it in order to feel recovered from her negative past.
She had to put her plan into motion now. She also knew that at
any moment, Byron was capable of doing something stupid that
would send her off.

Chapter 13

"Why don't you give her a job, Decorey, so she can leave?" Byron suggested, as he cleaned the mustard greens that were in the kitchen sink.

"No, she's been through a lot already in her life, and I'm not going to have her out there like that. Not just yet, Byron. We have to stick to our plan. Besides, you already know what the plan is for her, right? Wait a minute. Do you hear that?"
Byron smacked his lips and turned off the faucet. "No, what am I suppose to be hearing?"
"That moaning. I think Ciara is having another nightmare."
"I hate that dirty bitch, Dee!"
"Shut up! Let me see what's wrong with this damn girl."
Decorey slowly walked into the pitch-black bedroom where Ciara was. Her eyes were closed but her face was scrunched up in a hard grimace.
"Ciara, snap out of it!"
She didn't respond to Decorey's deep voice. Instead, her moaning continued until Byron splashed a cup of cold water onto her face.
Startled, Ciara jumped out of the bed dripping water onto the floor. "What happened?"
"You were having another nightmare. Maybe you need to talk about what's bothering you so much. You can't keep all of that

misery bottled inside that little body of yours, woman."
"She's okay. She needed some water on her ass anyway. The
damn room is starting to smell like feet and booty. Haven't you
ever heard of Summer's Eve?"
"Byron, could you please go back into the kitchen. I'm sure she
doesn't want to hear your smart-ass comments right now."
     "Whatever!" Byron said, twirling his hand in the air.
     "Ciara, why don't you get yourself cleaned up. I have
something important to talk to you about after lunch."
"Is it good or bad?"
"Bad!" Byron yelled from the other side of the door.
"Never mind him. I just need to talk to you about something."
"Cool, just let me get myself together and I'll be out there."
Ciara watched Decorey as he left the room. She didn't trust
them, and she still couldn't figure out from where she knew
Byron. All she knew was that she ran into the man before. She
heard the brothers preparing lunch in the kitchen and thought
they were about to give her a good riddance speech along with a
packed doggie bag. But, she was going to get them before they
got her. She had no plans on leaving that house empty-handed.
Byron was walking out of the front door with his car keys, and
Decorey was setting the table. Byron's bedroom was right
across from the one Ciara was sleeping in, so she slowly opened
the bedroom door, trying not be detected. She knew they had
some cash somewhere in that house, and now it was her
business to find it.
During previous searches while Decorey and Byron weren't
home, she had been unsuccessful in finding any money. She
didn't even find a bank statement or receipt.
     Ciara slowly crept into Byron's room and quietly closed the
door. His room looked as if he was preparing for a "Sweet 16"
party. His walls were painted pink and purple. One wall was

covered with different types of designer hats, and the other walls had posters and sticky notes on them. His purple rug co-ordinated well with his purple sheet set. It was funny because his room wasn't that clean for him to nag Ciara about her cleanliness. It was actually junky. He had a lot of empty Grey Goose bottles on the floor and on his dresser. His trash was overflowing with candy wrappers and used paper towels.

And he calls himself a homosexual, Ciara thought.

She tiptoed towards his closet and quietly searched through his belongings. There was nothing normal about his things.

"Bingo!" Ciara exclaimed, forgetting she was trying to be quiet and go undetected.

There was a brown gym bag under some clothes in the back of Byron's closet. She almost screamed when she saw the bundles of money inside. Quickly, she grabbed two bundles of tens and twenties, before zipping the bag back closed.

It had to have been around four or five thousand dollars in it. She dropped the money down in her jogging pants and pushed the bag back under the clothes in the closet. She returned to her room unnoticed and started counting the money.

"Ciara, are you ready to eat?"

Decorey's voice startled her.

"Yeah, just give me a little more time."

She grabbed the family-size bag of Doritos off of her bed and emptied the chips into the trash basket that was by the foot of her bed. She then placed the money into the bag and unlocked the bedroom window. After cautiously looking around to make sure no one was outside, she climbed out the first floor window and placed the bag under some fallen leaves that were piled up on the side of the house.

Ciara had a nice amount of getaway money if and when they asked her to leave the house. She climbed back in the window and began to prepare for lunch. *Don't fuck with me,* thought, while staring at her bedroom door.

******

"Thank you for the lunch, Decorey. I really do appreciate everything you're doing for me."
"Don't get use to it because you'll be leaving real soon," Byron mumbled.
"Don't start now, Byron," Decorey said, cutting his eyes at him.
"You know what? I really don't have time for your shit today, Byron!" Ciara yelled.
"Oh yeah? Well, I thought you would have plenty of time, with your unemployed ass."
"Hey, stop with all of this small talk so we can discuss business!" Decorey demanded.
"I'm sorry, Decorey, but Byron needs to watch his dick-sucking mouth!"
"Well, at least I suck better dick than you. Now what do you have to say about that, bitch?"
"So you're telling me that you're proud of the fact that you can suck dick better than a woman?" Ciara said, laughing cynically.
"Fuck you!"
Ciara ignored Byron's last comment. She didn't care anymore about being kicked out because she had the money waiting for her on the side of the house.
"So what is it that you want to talk about, Decorey?"
"I wanted to offer you a job working for me," he said in a low voice.
Ciara's eyes lit up. "Sure, what kind of work is it?"
"Well, I wouldn't call it *work*. It's more like paying off a debt."
"What are you talking about?"
"Relax, Ciara, because you really don't have a choice. This is a

life or death situation."

"Life or death? Decorey, I don't know what you're on, but I'm not understanding none of this."

"I told you that she wasn't going to agree with it."

"I'm leaving because this is some bullshit!" Ciara said, as she stood up from the table.

"Sit your ass down!" Decorey screamed, then pulled a black 9-millimeter from under his shirt.

Ciara slowly sat back down, staring at the black pistol that was a couple of feet from her.

"Besides, you and Shawn owe me."

"What? Owe you? What are you talking about? How do you know Shawn? That was my husband, and he's dead!"

"I know Shawn is dead, you fucking bitch!"

Decorey slapped Ciara with the butt of the pistol, and she fell to the floor holding her mouth. The blood seeped through her fingers as she tried to get up.

"Shawn was the first and last guy I ever had feelings for. He made me feel special, and when you came into the damn picture, he forgot all about me. Shawn treated me like I didn't exist. We were in a relationship, and he left me for you. I tried my best to get over him, but he didn't give me any closure. For years, I stalked and watched the two of you grow as a couple. The shit made me sick to my stomach. I always wondered what it was about you that swept him off his feet. Was the answer between your legs or did you have a good head on your shoulders, hoe? I didn't know you personally, but I knew you owed me for taking Shawn away from me. That's when I started to plot my revenge."

"But, I don't have anything to do with you and Shawn. I didn't even know Shawn was gay," Ciara painfully cried.

"Well, now you know. Shawn was a selfish, sneaky bastard that wanted everything his way. I knew he would never be faithful to me, but I never imagined him leaving me for a ghetto-ass bitch like you. I tried to delete Shawn from my memory, but he came back into my life when he started dating my friend Patrice. You may know her as Pink.

"Pink?" Ciara repeated.

"Pink was the stripper that Shawn left you for. What goes around comes around, Ciara. You took Shawn from Decorey, and she took Shawn from you, bitch," Byron said, as he lit a scented candle that was on the counter.

"This whole time y'all were playing me for a fool?"

"No, Ciara, you were playing yourself. If you never came into the picture, none of this would've happened. Pink told me everything about her relationship with Shawn. She was really in love with him. I was in a tough spot. I wanted to tell her about our past, but I knew she'd never believe me."

"I don't want to hear anymore of this. Just stop!"

"No, I can't just stop. Just like I couldn't stop loving Shawn when you invaded our world. He wouldn't even look at me again. He stopped answering my calls, and he even blocked me from sending him emails. Shawn just cut me off completely. He even started fucking my little brother behind my back."

Byron smiled as she glanced over at him. "Remember when I came to your house that day, Ciara?"

"I knew I'd seen you before somewhere," she said. "I just couldn't figure out which hoe stroll you were on."

"Bitch, you ain't never seen me on any stroll. You must have me mixed up with your momma, hoe!"

Sweat began to trickle down Byron's face.

"Don't get mad now, fag. My mother doesn't have anything to do with this."

"Fag? But this fag had your man, bitch!" Byron shot back,

snapping his fingers in her face. "And by the way, I loved the way Shawn's dick use to curve into my mouth. I told you that I suck dick better than you!"

Before Byron could say another word, Ciara jumped across the table and grabbed him. "You fucking punk! I'll kill you!"

Ciara had Byron by his neck. She was too overpowering for him. As much as he tried, he couldn't escape her grip.

"Shoot her, Decorey!" Byron pleaded in between gasping for air.

Decorey yanked her away from his brother, but she still managed to get one last hit in. Ciara lifted her right leg up in the air with as much force as she could muster and kicked Byron in his "I can suck dick better than you" lips.

"Get the fuck out of my house!" Decorey screamed, as he pointed the gun at Ciara.

Byron was still on the floor holding his mouth with a hand full of blood. Decorey grabbed Ciara and dragged her by her tangled hair to the front door. He pushed her so hard that she fell down the front steps backwards.

"I should've shot you for kicking my brother, bitch, but I didn't want to waste my bullets on a homewrecker like you." Decorey slammed the door.

"Fuck you! I hope you bitches get hit by a car while you're walking down the street in the gay parade, fags!" she screamed at the closed door.

Ciara got up and dusted her clothes off. Looking around, she noticed some neighbors outside.

"What the fuck is you looking at? You act like you never seen a bitch get kicked out before!"

She went to the side of the house to get her money from under the leaves. "Where the hell is my money?

The Doritos bag was gone. The money was gone. Her hopes

were gone.

"Shit! Somebody saw me put that money under here!"

Ciara kicked through the pile of leaves, but the money was nowhere to be found. She couldn't go back inside the house to get what little money she had been saving or her stuff. Once again, it was time for her to find another way.

She walked sullenly down the block to the bus stop, hoping she could catch the next one coming. When she made it to the bus stop, she reached into her pocket to see if she had enough change for the fare and a napkin to wipe the blood from her busted lip. Before she knew it, two squad cars pulled up next to her.

"Get on the fucking ground!" one officer yelled, as he pulled out his gun.

"What's going on?" Ciara fell to the ground. "Not so hard, officer," she begged, while the officer applied pressure to her back with his knee.

"Shut the fuck up!" the white officer screamed, as he vigorously placed Ciara's hands behind her back.

"I didn't even do anything!" she cried.

"Shut the fuck up, you damn crackhead! We got a complaint that you were bothering people in the neighborhood!"

"I just came outside, officer! I didn't do anything!"

"I said shut the fuck up!"

The police handcuffed Ciara and threw her into the back of the all-white unmarked Chevy Impala. At that point, everybody was coming outside to gawk at the apprehended person.

"That's a damn shame. Some things never change around here," an elderly man said, while wiping off the white walls on his Deville.

Ciara was broke, on the streets, and possibly going back to jail. Her heart was numb and her eyes were dry. Having gone through too much over the years, Ciara was unable to feel or cry anymore. She'd had enough of her life and was willing to trade her soul to the devil to get a new one. The next chance she got, she was going to make that happen.

Chapter14

Ciara gently rubbed her wrist as the scruffy looking police officer removed the tight handcuffs and directed her inside of the holding cell. She glanced around as she sat down next to a woman that was humming and rocking back and forth.

"Did you know I was the first person in Chicago to eat Harold's chicken before he became famous? Yes, it was me, baby!" the woman boasted.

Ciara looked over at the deranged woman, who started to hum again with her eyes closed.

What the hell is she talking about? Ciara thought, as she got up and walked to the other end of the cell.

It really didn't matter where Ciara sat, because the entire cell smelled like piss and fish. The walls were covered with dried blood and spit. The floor was cold, and the florescent light that dangled from the ceiling only lit up half of the cell.

"You can't sit there," a Hispanic woman in a torn dress said before Ciara's butt touched the wooden bench.

Ciara had to say something back to the woman. If she didn't, they would take her as being soft and test her for the duration of her time there.

"I don't give a fuck whose seat it is, bitch," Ciara retorted, staring at the woman with rage in her eyes.

Her heart sped up its pace when the large woman stood up from the bench exposing her Latin Queen tattoos that were on her arms. Latin Queens is the toughest and most feared female gang

Steven Morgan

in Chicago, and Ciara didn't want to have anything to do with the drama they could bring to her.

"She just got in here and you fools are at it already," the woman leaning against the wall opposite of Ciara yelled.

The obese Hispanic just walked away without saying another word to Ciara. The only reason she decided to walk away, though, was because one of the police officers walked by the cell. Other than that, the Latin Queen would've given Ciara a run for her money in the confined cell.

Ciara looked over at the lady who had spoken up for her and nodded her head, thanking the lady for saving her ass.

"Hey, what's your name?" the woman asked, walking towards Ciara.

"Ciara, and yours?"

"My name is Tasha. Are you from around here?"

Ciara didn't hear her response because she was too busy examining the woman's swollen lip and black eye.

"I'm sorry, what did you say your name was again?" Ciara apologetically asked.

"It's okay. I'm going to kill that nigga when I get out of here!" Tasha angrily said.

"What are you talking about?"

"My name is Tasha Mays, but I know you were looking at my face. My coward-ass boyfriend beat me up because I came home late from the club last night. This fool comes in every night drunk and high, and I don't say shit! But the one night I want to hang out and have some fun, he goes into Ike Turner mode on my ass. He thinks he owns me. He got me fucked up with them other sideline hoes he be messing with in the street."

Tasha was a fairly pretty woman. If it wasn't for the black eye and swollen lip, she would've been pretty damn sexy. Tasha was about 5'5" and 175 pounds. Some would consider her to be a full-figured woman, but she was well proportioned. She had short light brown hair, dark brown eyes, deep attractive dimples, and a tattoo on her neck that said "Diva". A star in her own way, but her boyfriend made sure she didn't shine too bright.

"I got tired of him beating on me, so I stabbed him while he was asleep!" Tasha admitted.

Damn, this girl went all psycho on the nigga when he was sleep, Ciara thought, as Tasha continued to talk.

"I mean, he didn't die or nothing, but I wanted him to, girl," Tasha continued. "I only stabbed him in his leg, but I should've cut off his fucking dick, like that white bitch Loraine Bobby, or whatever her name is, did. So now, I'm here because he pressed charges on me like a little bitch. After all the shit I've done and been through for him!"

Ciara could feel Tasha's pain in her voice. However, she didn't understand why this strange woman felt the need to confide in her.

"But I got something for his ass when I get out of here." Tasha could taste her revenge as she bit her bottom lip.

Damn, that's deep as hell, Ciara thought.

"Enough about my petty problems. Why are you in here?"

Ciara began to laugh.

"What's so damn funny?" Tasha asked.

"I beat up this gay dude and kicked about four of his teeth out."

"What!" Tasha said with a smile. "Now you know you can't just go around kicking out people's teeth."

The two women looked at each other and shared a small piece of a bond. For some reason, Tasha reminded Ciara of Kim. Maybe Ciara felt that way because Kim's birthday was only two days away. Either way, Ciara met someone that she liked and maybe could grow to trust.

For the rest of the night, Ciara and Tasha exchanged stories and watched out for each other, while the other women talked amongst themselves.

******

Steven Morgan

The next morning, Ciara was scheduled to face the judge. Since this was a minor offense, the most she would be faced with is three months of probation tops.
"I hope they don't try to keep me here?" Ciara whispered to Tasha.
"He didn't die, girl. He just can't smile for a while. You just remember what I told you. Go to my mother's house and wait for me to get there. I should be out tomorrow after I see the judge and post bail."
"Tasha, you tried to kill him! They're not going to let you out that easy."
"He beat me up, so I had to defend myself. That's what I'm going to tell the judge in the morning. Trust me, I have it all figured out."
"Blackwell!" the officer yelled, as he waited for the cell gate to completely open.
Ciara stood up and turned around so the officer could tightly secure the handcuffs on her wrists.
"When I get released, I'm going straight to your mother's house."
Being able to go to Tasha's mother's house was a blessing, especially since she had nowhere else to go.
"Okay, I'll see you later, and tell my mother that I said hi."
"Close it!" the officer yelled.
Ciara slowly walked in front of him down the hall. As they entered the packed courtroom, Ciara immediately looked to see if the judge was a man or woman.
Ciara's only defense tactic, at the moment, was to give the judge the most sweet and innocent look she could. She took a seat next to the other women who were waiting to see the judge.
Ciara's case was the first one called.
"Ciara Blackwell!" the bailiff shouted.
The judge picked up the paperwork in front of him and closely

examined the statement that was written down about Ciara. "What do you have to say about this inappropriate behavior of yours, Mrs. Blackwell?"

"I'm so sorry, and I do apologize for being the problem and not the solution, sir."

The judge slowly removed his glasses. "I've been a judge for twenty-nine years, and I have never heard that one before, Mrs. Blackwell. I like that response. Due to the fact that I'm feeling good today and the individual that pressed charges against you isn't here, consider yourself lucky, Mrs. Blackwell. Case dismissed!"

Ciara was escorted from the courtroom and placed into another room while she waited to be released, which took about six hours. When she stepped to the desk to retrieve her things, all of it was not there.

"I had some money in my pants. Where's my money?" Ciara questioned.

"Lady, I don't have your money. Now get out of my face!" the officer behind the desk said, as he handed Ciara her belongings.

"I guess you heard that one before, huh?"

"At least a million times."

The man didn't even give Ciara eye contact. He just continued reading his newspaper.

As another officer escorted her to the front building, he said, "Hey, shorty, you think I can get that number before you leave?"

"What? I don't even have an address. I'm homeless!"

"That's cool. We can take care of that later, sexy. I have plenty of room at my place. I live by Goose Island."

"Thanks, but no thanks," she replied. *I'm looking like a panhandler and this fool is thirsty for some ass,* she thought, then added, "Don't you have some police duties or something to take care of?"

"So it's like that?"

Steven Morgan

"It's just like that, off-i-cer!" Ciara slowly said. "I just want a hot shower and a plate of food, if you don't mind."

"Fuck you, jailbird!" The tall, black police officer reached into his pocket and threw seventy cents on the ground, then went back into the building.

Ciara never wanted to face that place again and didn't look back as she reached the bus stop that was across the street. She leaned against the nearest pole, watching people as they sped past her in their cars. It seemed as though they all had an important place to be and at a certain time. Maybe time was only at a standstill for her.

She saw every car that she ever wanted just driving by, leaving her behind. Previously, her life was about catering to her promiscuous husband and hanging with her best friend. Now, she wanted and needed things to be different. She wasn't going to be stupid again. It was her time to be selfish, and she was about to get everything she wanted. And getting money was going to help her start a new life.

About ten minutes later, the bus came and Ciara headed to Tasha's house. She could see the divergence in the neighborhood as she rode on the bus from the city into the suburb of Oak Park. Although only blocks separated the Westside from the Oak Park neighborhood, there was a noticeable change between the two areas.

Damn, I hope this lady doesn't come out snapping on me, Ciara thought as she got off the bus near Tasha's house.

She slowly walked up to the brick two-flat building and peeped through the curtains that were open, but she didn't see anyone.

"Yeah, who is it?" a woman asked from the other side of the door before she could even knock.

"Ciara Blackwell."

"Who?"

"Um, I'm Tasha's friend, Ciara."

The screen door opened and a large black woman stood in the

doorway trying to hold her robe closed with one hand. Ciara almost laughed, because Tasha's mother looked just like the lady from the *Tom and Jerry* cartoon.

"Come on in, baby. Tee-Tee told me all about you when she called this morning. She got into some trouble the other day, messing with that lowlife boyfriend of hers. I don't know what exactly happened, but I do know she needs to stop seeing that damn fool. I don't know what you girls see in those flashy punks."

Ciara didn't respond.

"Do you want something to drink or eat, baby?"

Tasha's mother was so polite. Although, she was wearing a house robe that was dirty and too small for her, she still made Ciara feel welcomed.

"Yeah, I'll take something to drink, ma'am."

"Well, we only have tap water and orange juice."

"I'll take some orange juice, ma'am."

"No, baby, don't call me ma'am anymore. It makes me feel old as hell. Just call me Momma or Ms. Mays."

"Oh, I'm so sorry, Ms. Mays," Ciara said in a soft tone.

"Don't be sorry. I know your folks raised you right. You need to rub some of that goodness off on my baby Tee-Tee when she makes it home. Where are you from, Ciara?"

Out of nowhere, a voice came from in the dining room.

"Look at that sweet tender thing right there!" the old man said, standing in the doorway of the dining room in his bright orange sweater.

"Earl, don't come in here and start messing with that girl. She's here for Tasha."

"Woman, I ain't doing nothing. I just like what I see."

The old man walked into the room with suspenders and jeans on. Ciara thought he must be from the Deep South.

"Don't pay him any attention, Ciara. That's just my old and crazy brother, Earl."

Steven Morgan

"Old? The car may be old, but it still starts up. If you know what I mean," Earl said, winking at Ciara.

"Sit your drunk ass down somewhere. You're an old perverted fool!"

"Stop yelling at me, woman, and go clean up or something!"

"It's my house to live in, not yours. If I wanted to, I could shit on the floors."

Ciara didn't know if she should laugh or move out of the way of the family feud.

"Whatever, you never let me have any fun in here."

"You don't need to have any fun, old man. Go and take your damn medication. I'll be glad when the good Lord invites you home."

"Oh, you'll see His house before I do, hag!"

Earl grabbed a pen and piece of paper off of the coffee table and started to write something down.

"Here you go, sweet thing. Call me sometime. I don't bite. At least not all the time," Earl said, as he grabbed the *Chicago Sun-Times* newspaper off of the table and left the room.

Later on that night, Tasha's mother made up a nice bed for Ciara in the guestroom.

"Now, Tasha should be here soon. I think she said she goes to court in the morning, and they should release her around noon."

"Okay, thank you for everything. I really do appreciate it."

"Goodnight, baby. I'll see you in the morning," Tasha's mother said, then closed the bedroom door behind her.

Ciara sat down on the edge of the soft queen-size bed and began to think about Shawn and Kim, while holding the only two pictures she had of them.

Thoughts of regret, love, and pain swirled in Ciara's head. Could she have been a better wife? Is that why Shawn stepped out on her with Pink? How could he have loved someone else, especially a man? She longed for the answers that would help her find closure, but she knew she would never get them. Instead, she had to love Shawn and Kim despite all of the backstabbing, cheating, and fighting. She did love them, and she truly missed their presence in her life.

Ciara looked over at the digital clock sitting on the nightstand.

"Happy birthday, Kim. I know you would've celebrated in style," she said in remembrance of her partner in crime.

She kissed the pictures just before placing them back into her bag. Just then, Decorey and Byron popped into her head. They may have thought they got the best of her, but she was ready to wreak the same havoc on their lives as they did hers and Shawn's.

Ciara pulled the covers back on the bed and yawned as she laid her body down. She stared at the ceiling full of stars and other glow-in-the-dark objects until she felt herself dozing off. This was the first time in years she felt safe and at ease.

The next morning, Ciara woke up out of her deep sleep and heard Fred Hammond's music playing throughout the house with the smell of fresh coffee brewing in the kitchen. Her body felt rested and relaxed as she stretched. She looked around the room when she got out of the bed and walked towards the window. In the view from the window, Tasha walked from across the street towards the house. Taking a quick look into the mirror that was behind the closet door, she put her hair into a ponytail and left the room.

As Ciara bounced down the stairs, the front door opened. "Hey Tasha," Ciara said, as she reached the last step on the staircase.

"I thought you weren't going to come here," Tasha replied in an excited voice.

"I told you I was coming. What made you think I wouldn't?"

"I don't know, but I'm glad you're here because we have some business to take care of. After I take a shower and get dressed, we can talk about everything."

Steven Morgan

Tasha's mother walked into the room with a fresh pot of coffee in her hand.

"Look at my precious Tee-Tee."

"Ma, please stop calling me Tee-Tee," Tasha replied, as she tried to straighten her clothes.

"Are you okay, baby? They didn't try to touch on you or nothing, did they?"

"I'm okay. Stop treating me like a little girl, Ma. I know how to handle myself."

"Hush up, child. You'll always be Momma's little girl. Now come on in the kitchen and get some of these hotcakes."

"Hotcakes? I'm all for a plate or two of hotcakes, Ms. Mays," Ciara said, rubbing her stomach.

"Ciara, I thought we were going to discuss our business?"

"We are, but I haven't had pancakes in years."

"Let the child get something to eat, Tee-Tee, while you go and get yourself together. Come on in here and sit down, Ciara. I'll make you a plate in no time at all."

Tasha left the two women in the kitchen and went upstairs to unwind. She cleaned the tub and ran the water for her overdue soaking. She carefully kneeled down, but felt pain in her lower back as she leaned over the edge of the claw-foot tub. Her back was still severely bruised from her fight with her boyfriend.

Tasha made it back downstairs just as Ciara was finishing up her glass of O.J.

"Damn, Ciara, I see you got your grub on," Tasha said.

"Yeah, everything was on point, too. I had eggs, hash browns, bacon, wheat toast, and pancakes. Your mother can really cook some pancakes."

"I know. I've been eating like that for years. That's why my ass is spreading now," Tasha said. She tried to prove a point by grabbing her own booty.

"You ready to talk business?"

"Yeah, let's go out back," Tasha replied.

Tasha looked around for her mother and motioned Ciara to follow her. Ciara stood up from the table and examined Tasha from head to toe. Tasha had on some orange and white Jordan's, with the matching orange and white Rocawear outfit. An orange scarf covered her hair, and every time she took a step, you could smell her Wild Honeysuckle lotion in the air. Tasha's appearance made her want to step up her game. Ciara wasn't usually the one to let another female outshine her.

They got a safe distance away from Tasha's mother's ears before they began to speak.

"Ciara, I know we just met, but I feel like I can trust you on this one. I want to rob my boyfriend. I hate that motherfucker, and I have to pay him back for all the shit he's done to me."

Ciara knew Tasha and her boyfriend had issues, but she didn't think they were this bad. She was eager to hear more.

"Okay, how do you plan on doing that? I'm down for it, but I want to make sure everything is planned out first."

"It's easy. All we have to do is put a woman in his face, and he's going to be vulnerable as hell. That's where you come into the picture. I don't want anyone else in on this but us. I just need you to start fucking with this dummy. I'm done dealing with him. I can't keep covering up black eyes and bruises for the rest of my life. I just can't go through it anymore."

"I feel you, girl. So what do you want me to do?"

"I want you to talk to him and go out with him. You know, the whole nine. He has a little money from hustling, and I want it all."

Ciara's eyes lit up. This was just the type of business she was trying to be on. Now she had someone who could help her make it happen.

"How much money are you talking about?"

"He's a small-time hustler. At the most, he might have about twenty-five stacks to his name. That's twelve and a half a piece.

Steven Morgan

It's not much, but it's something to work with for now. We have to hit the mall and get your wardrobe together first. He really doesn't mess with chicks that don't have their shit together. I'm not saying that you're looking like a bum, but from all the times I've caught him cheating, the females had it going on."

"I don't have any money," Ciara shamefully replied.

"Don't worry. I have a little money to play with. I always use to pinch off of that nigga's money when he told me to count it. Like Jay-Z said, 'Put a little in the baggie…put a little in the purse'. Do you smoke weed?"

"Is an elephant heavy?"

"Okay, that's what I'm talking about. I know somebody who has some Kush. We can get some on the way to the mall."

Tasha and Ciara drove around for a while, but they didn't have luck finding any Kush on the streets.

"Fuck this. I need some weed, but I'm not going to pay for some regular-ass weed."

Just as Tasha began to complain again, her cell phone started ringing.

"Here's the dude with the Kush right here, Ciara. What's up, Ronnie? You got something good for me?"

"Yeah, what's good, sexy?"

"Let me get three for fifty."

"I can't do that one. You know it's a drought right now. But my guy got some good mid grade down the street. He stays in K-town on Kilpatrick. I can hit him real fast if you want me to."

"I'm good on that regular, Ronnie. I'll just get some of what you got. Where do you want me to meet you?"

"Meet me on Central and Madison in ten minutes."

"Okay, ten minutes, but what car are you in?"

"I'm in my baby's momma's car. You know, the silver Monte Carlo with the 22's."

"I'll be there in ten minutes. Don't have me waiting for you all day."

"Calm down. I'm on my way right now."

Tasha hung up and placed her cell phone on her lap. "Fuck that nigga Ronnie. I'm going to go and get his guy's weed on Kilpatrick. I know where they be hustling at over there. Ronnie always be yelling that drought shit when I call him."

"I thought you said you weren't gonna pay for some regular green?"

"I'm not, Ciara. I'm gonna take his whole pack. You ain't scared are you? I'll take you home if you're scared," Tasha jokingly asked.

"First of all, this ain't *Belly*, and I'm not scared of shit. I just don't want to be bothered with them K-town dudes. You know they be on some wild shit."

"It's all good. Stop acting like you a suburban chick. Just sit back and watch how I hit this easy lick."

Tasha slowly turned her black Grand Prix down Kilpatrick Street. On one end of the block, fiends were lined up trying to get the free drugs that the hustlers gave out when they got new product in. On the other end, younger hustlers in all-white tees were passing out sacks of weed like free turkeys on Thanksgiving Day.

"They should be right down here."

When Tasha pulled up behind a gray Tahoe that was parked in front of the weed spot, a young worker ran from the porch with his hands in his pockets.

"What you trying to get, shorty?" the young hustler asked, while trying to see who Ciara was in the passenger seat.

"Why are you out here hustling, Marco? You look like a baby out here with all these older dudes."

"I'm trying to get it. You know how it is, baby. We're trying to eat out here. But forget about all of that. What are you trying to grab?"

"Let me see what the weed looks like."

Steven Morgan

"Why? It looks just like it did the last time you bought a sack."

"Just let me see the jab, Marco," Tasha demanded.

Marco looked around to see if any undercover cars were riding through the block.

"Here you go." He handed Tasha the whole zip of weed.

"Thanks," Tasha said, then rolled up the window and pulled off.

"What the fuck!" Marco ran back to the porch to grab his thumper from the bushes, but Tasha was already down the block and turning the corner. He tried to get a good shot, but she was too far.

"Hold on, lil man, it's too many people out here. Put that fuckin' gun away. You tryin' to bring heat to the trap over some bitches?" Big Lord advised.

"Man, that bitch took my whole jab!"

The fat man didn't let the conversation interrupt the counting of the fat knot of money in his hand. "That's on you, homie. Now straighten up. You have to go and work some happies now."

Marco didn't want to work for free, but he didn't have a choice.

The man handed Marco another ounce of weed and walked to his car. Marco took the work and went back to his post, protesting. He was still looking in the direction that Tasha and Ciara went in.

"I'm going to get that bitch. Watch and see. I'll see those hoes again."

"I told you it was a sweet lick," Tasha bragged. She handed Ciara the bag of weed and sped through a narrow alley. "Damn, this shit smells good, too. I feel like a fat kid in a candy store."

The marijuana aroma coming from the bag reminded Ciara of her smoking sessions she shared with Kim. The harder she tried to distance herself from the past, the more it snuck up in her thoughts and life.

After an hour of smoking and plotting, the duo had a plan to work with. Tasha knew Desmond was weak for women, and he would leave himself open for betrayal just for a quick taste or smell of a fine woman.

Desmond wasn't your typical hustler. He was more of a part-time hustler. He would tell Tasha that he had business to take care of in the streets, but that was the excuse he used to go be with other women. He really only hustled when he lost money gambling. The reason he had some money is because he ran with some real go-getters that put him onto different hustles. He was a real doughboy at 5'7" and 275 pounds. He was fat, black, and ugly as ever with braids, but he never stayed Coogi down to the socks. He wore white tees and jeans every day. The swagger that a lot of street dudes possessed, he lacked. The thoroughbred heart, he lacked that, as well. The only reason he was able to get the pussy he did get was because he didn't mind tricking off his money.

A lot of people around the way knew Desmond was soft because he never took care of any beef that he had in the streets himself. He always ran to his uncle Chris for protection. His uncle was a high-ranking, five-star, elite gangster disciple. He was known for shooting first and asking questions last. He was the main reason why Desmond didn't have any worries in the streets. However, Tasha and Ciara planned on changing that real soon. Desmond was an easy target because he would never expect Tasha to pay him back like this.

About two weeks went by and the plan began to go into full affect. Ciara was introduced to Desmond through a mutual friend that Tasha and Desmond both knew.

Chapter 15

The clean, baby blue, box Chevy Caprice slowly cruised down the street while onlookers followed Desmond's sparkling Lowenhart rims to the end of the block. The cool evening breeze flowed through the custom t-top Chevy, as Desmond tried his best to entertain his sexy passenger.

"You don't talk much, huh? You haven't said one word since we left the restaurant. You want to watch TV or something?" Desmond asked.

As the seven-inch screen popped up from the radio, Ciara noticed a group of guys that were trying to get her attention as they waited at the stoplight.

"Shorty, can I holler at you for a minute?" one of the men yelled from the backseat of a pearl white, newer model Escalade.

"No, thank you. I'm straight," she said, waving to the bold passenger.

"It's like that, shorty? I'm not about to sweat you!" the man shot back.

"Good, nigga! You can keep it moving!" Desmond courageously yelled to the man.

Desmond was all bark and no bite. The only reason he said something in response to the man is because Ciara was in the car. He didn't want her to think he was weak and couldn't hold his own out there in the streets.

"What? Fat boy, ain't nobody even talking to you. You

better calm the fuck down before we snatch you up out of that ugly-ass car," the driver retorted.

"Just pull off, Desmond. It's not even worth it. Those fools are looking to get into some trouble. Let's just go," Ciara suggested. She grabbed his rusty hand, trying to persuade him to end the pointless conversation.

Desmond knew the situation could get ugly if he tried to test the group of aggressive men. While looking over at them, he pulled off when the light turned green. He carefully watched the men in his rearview mirror as they turned down a side street that was a block away from the light. All Desmond had to do was make a phone call to his uncle and all of his worries in the street were over, just like that.

"Can I ask you a question? Why is it that you don't have a woman?" Ciara asked, as she played with the different functions on the Clarion TV radio.

"I don't know. I just haven't found her yet," Desmond lied. *What about Tasha?* Ciara thought.

"Okay, what about friends? Every man has a friend or two."

"I have a few prospects, but nothing serious. To be honest, I really don't have time for a woman. You females play too many games, and I don't have time for that. I'm trying to get my money right. After I do that, then I might choose one."

Choose one? Ciara repeated in her head, as she glanced over at her date in disbelief. He didn't sound right making a bold comment as he just did.

She eyed Desmond's mannerisms and attire. He wasn't in his everyday white t-shirt and jeans. He looked nice with his brown Prada shoes, dark blue Rocawear jeans, and brown Rocawear sweater. *Not bad at all*, Ciara thought, as she unwrapped a piece of Trident gum for her dry mouth.

As Desmond pulled into the Bar Louie tavern parking lot, Ciara performed a quick appearance check. Everything was in order. She was looking good as usual in her yellow and white Juicy Couture outfit, and Desmond surprisingly appeared to be on the same page for the moment. He got out of the car, stepping around to the passenger side to open her door. That was a first. They walked towards the door, arm in arm, but was stopped short of the entrance.

"I need to see two pieces of identification. Let's make this quick, because I don't have all night," the bouncer demanded, as he held his hand out waiting for his request.

"I don't have two pieces of ID. I don't have any ID on me. Damn, is a celebrity performing tonight? Is Michelle and Barack in there?" Ciara questioned, peeping around the bouncer's massive body.

"Those are the rules. I don't make them. I just enforce them. Understand?"

"Let's just go. It's obvious they don't want our money." Just then, Desmond pulled out a hand full of money, flashing it in the bouncer's stern face.

Ciara leisurely turned to follow him back to the Chevy, when the same Escalade with the rowdy group of guys turned into the lot. She recognized them instantly.

"Wait, Desmond. Those are the same crazy niggas we saw earlier. I don't want them to hear your car when you start it."

Desmond took his hand away from the key and watched each of the men walk into Bar Louie before driving off.

"What the fuck did I do now?" Desmond mumbled, reducing his speed after seeing the flashing lights of the police car in his rearview mirror.

"I hope you don't have any drugs on you." Ciara eased

into her seatbelt, trying not to be detected.

"It's all good. Just stay calm, and this will be over before you know it."

Desmond carefully pulled over, making sure he abided by all of the rules of the road in the process.

A million and one thoughts ran through his mind, while Ciara sat unfazed by the situation. He was uneasy because he didn't know if his license and registration were good or not. The cop took his time walking to the driver's window, and with each second, Desmond became more disturbed.

"Do you know why I pulled you over?"

"No, I do not, sir. Could you please inform me of what I've done?" Desmond respectfully asked the officer that was shining the black Pelican flashlight in his face.

Ciara continued to look straight ahead, not giving the officer any eye contact.

"You were going too fast when you came out of that parking lot back there. You didn't even stop to see if any cars were coming."

"I'm sorry, officer. Here's my license and insurance card, sir."

"I didn't ask you for that, but since you're volunteering, I guess I will run a quick check to see if you're clean," the officer laughed, as he grabbed Desmond's info and headed back towards his car.

"Why did you give him your ID before he asked for it, Desmond?"

"Because of Tasha's stupid ass," he angrily yelled.

"Tasha? Who's Tasha?" Ciara asked, pretending not to know.

"That's my girl. I mean, my ex-girlfriend. She still be tripping because I don't want her ass back. I'm going to kill that hoe when I see her!"

"So what does Tasha have to do with us getting pulled over right now? Is she an investigator or something?" Ciara tried her best to stifle a laugh.

"It's a long story! Just sit back and let me figure this shit out."

"It's nothing to worry about."

The officer didn't take long to get his results back from running Desmond's information.

"Everything is clean. Just slow it down, Pervis, and put on that seatbelt." The officer didn't bother to ask Ciara for her information since Desmond was clean.

"Your real name is Pervis?" Ciara snickered.

"Yeah, but keep that on the low. I promise I don't want any of those niggas from the block to know that. I'll be banned from the neighborhood," Desmond joked. However, there was some truth to that statement.

"Your secret is safe with me…Pervis!"

******

The drive back to Ciara's car was short, but talkative. Desmond was feeling comfortable around her, and they began telling jokes and talking about life. The anticipation of another date was definitely in the picture for the two of them, but Ciara and Desmond were expecting two different outcomes for the next date. He expected a night of passionate sex, and she expected to be counting money by the end of the date.

"I have some business to take care of tomorrow, but I would love to take you out again next week, if you're not busy. I already know you have niggas lined up waiting to be with you."

"No, it's not like that with me. I'll be glad to go out with you again. Just let me know when."

Ciara leaned over towards Desmond and kissed him on the cheek. When she got out of his car, she made sure her round ass swayed from side to side. There was one thing she knew about most men; they could not pass up a cute woman with a small waist and fat ass. Desmond watched her every move, while waiting for her to get in and start the engine before he sped away.

No sooner than his taillights faded away, Ciara was on the phone spilling the news to Tasha.

"So how did it go? What happened?" Tasha was anxious to know.

"First of all, calm down, girl. Nothing happened. We didn't even get a chance to go out. He claimed he had some business to take care of, but he asked to take me out next week."

"That's it? You didn't ask him about me or nothing?"

"You should've come with us if you're going to question me like this. Everything is cool. I know for sure he's a lame and this shouldn't be hard at all. I think we should make this happen next week when I go out with him. He won't even see it coming."

The plan was set in Ciara's mind, and she was going through with it. Hopefully, Tasha was ready, as well.

******

Desmond wanted to make sure everything was right for his second date with Ciara. They started off the date by attending a show at The House of Blues. Ciara had never been, so she was very impressed. Next, he reserved a room at the Hyatt Hotel, where they enjoyed a nice meal he picked up from the remarkable Alinea Restaurant in downtown Chicago. They shared a bottle of Remy Martin and chased it with Moet and strawberries. To enhance their buzz, they enjoyed numerous blunts of Ice weed that his uncle Chris got from California.

He was putting in that good ole' overtime work to make sure he saw her naked tonight. After great food and conversation, he presented her with a gift wrapped in the traditional brown and gold Gucci box. Inside was a pair of Gucci sandals with the matching wallet that cost him over six hundred dollars.

This would definitely piss off Tasha if she found out about it. The most expensive thing Desmond had bought for her was an Apple Bottoms outfit, and it was from Burlington Coat Factory. He couldn't even buy it at the full retail price at Macy's.

"Damn, that was good," he said, as he wiped his mouth with a napkin.

"Yeah, it was pretty good, Dez."

"Dez? Nobody calls me Dez. Is that my new nickname or something, shorty?"

Desmond's cell phone began to ring. He glanced at the caller ID and saw Tasha's name. Ciara looked over at the clock on the table; it was after one in the morning.

Perfect, Ciara thought, as she walked over to the other end of the room.

"What the hell does she want?" he said, sending the call to voicemail.

"Who is that?"

"No one important, baby." Before Desmond could press the power button on his cell phone, it began to ring again.

"Damn, I guess that person *is* important because they're calling again."

He didn't want Ciara to think another female was calling him while he was with her, but she already knew what was going on because the phone call was a part of their plan.

"Bitch, stop fucking calling me!" he yelled into the phone's receiver.

She knew Tasha would be calling Desmond's cell phone twice to let her know she was outside waiting. Ciara played her role perfectly.

"Forget about that stupid bitch. Let's talk about us." Desmond tossed his cell phone on the nightstand. "We've been talking for about three weeks now and I still haven't had a chance to kiss you."

Nigga, please. First of all, take some of that damn Chap Stick off, and do something with them old-ass braids, Ciara thought.

If he could hear what she was thinking, he would've slapped the shit out of her.

"I know, but I wanted to take things slow this time around. I really think you have the potential to be the one, and I'm not trying to give you any reason to think of me as one of these easy chicks out here," Ciara replied in her innocent voice.
"Easy? Now why would I think of you like that?" he said, exposing his large yellow teeth.
"I know you're use to females being all over you, but I'm not like that."

Desmond assumed that was his cue from Ciara. So, he came close to make his move. As he kissed her neck, he fondled her breast and worked his way to her mid-section. His seductive behavior made Ciara sick to her stomach. He slowly lifted her skirt, trying to gain easy access. After pulling down her panties and seeing her neatly trimmed pussy hairs, he immediately got an erection.

Just as he began to go down on her, someone knocked on the hotel room door. Desmond was upset that someone interrupted him while he was about to feast. He didn't even look through the peephole; it was a mistake that only a wannabe street nigga would make. He opened the door, in a rush to get back to Ciara, but came face to face with the barrel of Tasha's gun.

"What the fuck!" He looked back at Ciara, who had her pistol out, too. "You fucking bitches set me up! Y'all some stupid hoes! Wait until my uncle finds out about this!"

"Shut the fuck up, nigga!" Tasha slapped Desmond in the face with the butt of the gun.

He fell to the floor in pain, with blood and some of his teeth in his hand.

"You're one of those weak bastards that can hit on a woman but will get punked by another nigga!" Tasha lost control. She repeatedly hit Desmond with the gun on top of his head. Blood was everywhere. He was on the floor motionless.

"Tasha, stop!"

Ciara snatched the gun out of her hand, and Tasha fell to her knees crying. Every emotion she ever felt while in this relationship finally bubbled to the top and exploded. It was a mixture of pain, guilt, hurt, humiliation, and desperation; but it felt good to be able to get the best of that nigga.

"I think he's dead!" Ciara said, looking at the body lying on the floor.

"This motherfucker is not dead!" Tasha went over to kick his body, but Desmond didn't move. "Damn! I think he is dead."

"No shit!" Ciara replied. "Grab his house keys and let's go!"

Ciara picked up everything that she thought had her fingerprints on it, while Tasha grabbed the keys and went to the bathroom to wash her hands and face.

"We don't have time for that shit, Tasha. Let's go!"

Tasha turned off the water, and the two girls left the hotel room.

On the drive to Desmond's house, Ciara was quiet. She was thinking about the twenty-five thousand that Tasha said Desmond had stashed away. It didn't matter to her how Tasha felt or that Desmond was dead. Her only concern was getting her hands on the money.

Tasha drove the car into the alley directly behind Desmond's house.

"Let's make this quick. Who lives in those two houses right there?" Ciara asked, pointing at the neighbors' houses.

"No one lives over here and the old woman right there is out of town."

Inside the house, Tasha knew right where to go. They peeled up the carpet in the bedroom, exposing loose floorboards. Tasha removed three planks of wood that hid a small hole in the floor. Within five short, nervous seconds, she held an unknown amount of money in her hands.

Desmond had a lot of jewelry and electronics around the house, but they got what they came for and didn't want to be greedy. Ciara and Tasha were satisfied with the money and prepared to leave. Making sure they didn't leave a trace, Ciara sprayed Lysol and removed their fingerprints from the door handles. The women put the money inside of three pillowcases and quickly made it back to the car.

Tasha had a room at the Motel 6 that was about forty-five minutes from Desmond's house. At the motel, they counted out fifty-seven thousand dollars in cash. Ciara's heartbeat was pumping in overdrive. Having never been this close to such a large amount of money, it was actually somewhat orgasmic to her.

"We're rich!" Tasha yelled, then tossed a bundle of money in the air.

"Rich? We're nowhere near rich," Ciara said, raining on Tasha's parade. "This isn't shit."

"Girl, are you crazy? This is a lot of money!"

"This ain't shit because someone is dead. If someone had to die, we should have at least gotten more money."

"Damn, you're talking like you don't want your half or something."

"Oh, I'm getting my half. I just want to get more money. We need to double up." Ciara stared at the pile of money on the bed, plotting the next move.

"Well, how are we going to do that? I don't have any more ex-boyfriends to rob."

"Don't worry about who we're going to rob, Tasha. I just need to know if you're down with me through this. We need to have each other's back through the thick and thin. We're either gonna be in it all the way together or we part ways now."

"Of course, I am."

"Cool, that's all I needed to hear. We're gonna rape this town."

This was the opportunity Ciara had been waiting for. She finally found a hustle that would bring her a serious cash flow. All she needed was for Tasha to be down with what she had in mind. It was them against the streets and the weak.

******

The next morning, Ciara and Tasha left the hotel room and headed to Gary, Indiana, to lay low for a couple of weeks until the heat from Desmond's murder died down. They took twelve hundred dollars apiece to rent a hotel room and to buy a minivan that they would drive while in town.

This was as good of a time as any for Ciara and Tasha to figure out the next step and the next victim. Ciara's intuition warned her that she and Tasha were not on the same page. A happy medium had to be outlined now before they went on together.

"We have to figure out what our next move is before we go back, Ciara, because I don't want our next mission to end up like it did last night. I don't want anybody else to die."

"Die? That's a part of the game! If it goes down like that, so be it. How many people you think is going to let us rob them and walk away? None. So, we have to handle business no matter what the outcome may be. If you didn't want anyone to die, then why in the hell did you beat his ass to death?"

Tasha ignored Ciara's question.

"I'm about to get some sleep. Can you wake me up in two hours, if you're not gone?"

"I'll wake you up when I get back from the store," Ciara said.

As soon as she got inside the minivan, she reached into the ashtray and grabbed the half-finished blunt that was there. She slowly rotated the blunt between her index finger and thumb as she lit it. She inhaled deeply to immediately feel the effect of the marijuana. After finishing it, Ciara drove to the store that was down the street.

She tried to walk into the store, but a tall, well-dressed man was blocking the doorway, waiting for the grocery store worker to push a cart to him.

"Excuse me," Ciara said.

The man knew she was high as a kite from the heavy weed stench on her clothes and the bloody-red color of her eyes.

"I'm so sorry, beautiful," the man replied. His eyes darted across the voluptuous frame of Ciara's body.

"Thanks for nothing," she replied, walking past the well-mannered man.

"Have you ever been to Live for God Baptist Church?" the man quickly asked before the opportunity faded.

"Excuse me. Do I even know you?"

"I didn't mean to bother you, sister, but I just wanted to invite you to my church this Sunday. I'm Pastor Fabian Edwards of Live for God Baptist Church."

"So that's how you're able to dress so nice? You're taking those people's money and buying Armani suits and cars, huh?"

"Young sister, these are blessings from my God above!"

"Your God?" Ciara mockingly replied.

"At least take my card and think about it, young sister."

She took the card and walked away.

He couldn't take his gaze off of her backside. A pastor is just as human and flawed as any other man.

"Be careful with Pastor Edwards, girl," a lady said. She had been in the aisle pretending to look at the body wash, but listening to and watching the entire interaction between Ciara and the pastor.

Ciara looked around, not knowing if the strange woman was speaking to her. "Are you talking to me?"

"Yeah. Pastor Edwards has paid for more abortions than the law should allow. He invites young pretty girls like yourself to his church, and the next thing you know, they end up pregnant and the church has to start a collection to pay for it. He's attractive and all, but he isn't worth two shits. So, be careful."

"I'm not trying to mess with him. I'm not even from here, so that wouldn't apply to me."

"So why did you take his card? That's all a part of his game. He reels you in with the church invitation. Then the next thing you know, you're pregnant and he's on to the next victim."

"Damn, and he's still a pastor here in Gary?"

"He has one of the biggest followings in Indiana. His church collects about twenty thousand dollars each month. How do you think he has the Mercedes and fancy clothes?"

Ciara got the notion that the woman knew all of this information from a close, personal experience with the pastor and his church.

"Don't look at me like that. I know from firsthand experience. I'm just trying to lookout for you."

Ciara gave the woman a slight nod of her head and went on about her business. She was there to shop; she didn't feel like making friends with strangers. Once she exited the store, she pulled out the pastor's business card. Ciara studied every word and letter written on it, and a devilish smile crept across her lips. If the pastor really got down like the woman said, Ciara would be happy to be the one to teach him a lesson. She was eager to get back and tell Tasha that she found the source of their next meal ticket.

******

When Ciara made it back to the room, Tasha was just getting out of the shower and walking out of the bathroom, nude. Her nipples were hard from the cool air coming from the air conditioner. Ciara watched as she slowly rubbed the cocoa butter lotion on her legs. *Damn, she has a sexy body,* Ciara thought, while Tasha pulled up her Victoria's Secret panties over her butt. For some reason, the sight of Tasha's full-figured body aroused her. Ciara was never curious about other women, but there was something about Tasha that she was attracted to. However, this was not the time to satisfy her curiosity because she couldn't let anything distract her from what she was trying to accomplish. Ciara dismissed the thoughts from her mind and began to tell Tasha about the news.

"Girl, check this out. I just met this pastor, and he wants me to come to his church this Sunday. I think this is our next mission right here."

"Mission for what? I'm not about to rob a pastor. Do you know how wrong that is?"

"It can't be worse than killing Desmond," Ciara replied.

Tasha cut her eyes at Ciara. "I just don't think we should do it. Besides, how do you know he has money? And if he does, it's not going to be cash."

"That's why we're going to rob him at the end of the month at the church. That's when all of the money for the month is counted and prepared so they can deposit it. I have it all planned out."

"I still don't think it's a good idea. Let me think about it some more. I just don't want anyone to get hurt this time," Tasha said, as she grabbed some money from her bag.

Robbing her abusive ex-boyfriend was one thing, but going after strangers in another city was out of her league. Tasha was skeptical about robbing the pastor. She felt it was morally wrong, but she knew Ciara wasn't changing her mind no matter what. Tasha didn't have much time to think about it, though, because she knew Ciara would want to make it happen as soon as possible.

As soon as Tasha left the room, Ciara picked up the phone and called the pastor.

"God is good. This is Pastor Edwards. How may I help you?"

"Pastor Edwards, this is Ciara. I met you at the grocery store earlier today, and you invited me to your church this Sunday."

"Yes, I remember you, Ciara. How are you doing?"

"I'm okay. I just wanted to say thank you so much because I

do need to change some things in my life, and I think by me running into you today it was a sign from God."

"That's good to hear, young sister. I'll be honored to have you at my sermon this Sunday. Make sure you have on your best Sunday clothes, because I want to personally speak to you after the service is over."

I bet you do, you damn pervert, Ciara thought. "Okay, Pastor Edwards, I'll see you on Sunday."

"Have a good day, and may God bless you, Ciara," Pastor Edwards said before ending the call.

Ciara felt a wave of satisfaction flowing through her body. All she needed to do to get her hands on more money was plan accordingly, get Tasha's scary ass on board, and make the right moves.

******

Ciara was up early Sunday morning fixing her hair and packing her clothes. Tasha woke up, not knowing what was going on.

"What are you doing?" Tasha asked in between two big yawns.

"I'm getting ready. You should be up getting ready, too."
"I'm talking about why are you packing your clothes?"
"Tasha, we can't stay here anymore. After we handle this business, I'm driving back to Chicago."
"But I thought we were staying here until things calmed down in Chicago."
"I know, but we can't just stay here after we rob Pastor Edwards. He's going to send the feds after us!"
"So you're still going to do this? I thought we were just going to the church and that's it."

"Give me a good reason why I should just go to church, Tasha? I haven't been to church in twenty-six years, and I'm only twenty-seven. So, you do the math. I'm not trying to repent for nothing I've done. I'm going to get this money with or without you."

Tasha walked into the bathroom and splashed water onto her face.

"I'll be outside in the van. Hurry up," Ciara yelled from the other side of the bathroom door.

Tasha couldn't take her time and shower like she normally did since Ciara was in a rush, so she treated her shower like she was running late for work. She grabbed her body wash and face towel and showered in record-breaking time.

When she stepped out of the shower, she quickly found an outfit and got dressed before Ciara had time to come back in to check on her. She put on a beige dress with her matching beige three-inch heels. Since she couldn't find any clean thongs, she decided not to wear any. As she stepped outside, she saw Ciara applying make-up to her face while looking in the van's passenger side mirror.

"You look very nice, Tasha."

"Thanks. Are you ready to go?" she replied, not bothering to return the compliment to Ciara.

Tasha started the van and drove in the direction of the church. The only sounds coming from within the minivan was from the sweet and sultry voice of Beyoncé and an occasional direction from Ciara. Other than that, the women did not speak to one another on the drive there.

The church was a short distance from their motel, and when they pulled into the lot, they noticed there were only a couple of cars in the lot.

"I thought you said service was at one o'clock?"

"That's what Pastor Edwards told me."
After parking the van, the two went inside the church, where a custodian was vacuuming the floors.
"Is Pastor Edwards here?" Ciara asked the young man.
"He's in his office taking care of some paperwork. Do you want me to tell him that you're here?"
"That's alright. I'll just go back there. He's expecting us," Ciara answered.

Ciara and Tasha walked down the hallway and spotted Pastor Edwards' office on the right side of the hallway. Ciara pulled out her .22 caliber handgun and checked the clip before placing it back in her purse. Tasha was so nervous that sweat trickled down her face the closer they got to his office. Ciara slowly turned the knob and opened the door wide enough to get a sneak peep before she entered. Perfect! The victim was making this too easy, as he sat behind his grand desk counting money. She looked back at Tasha and smiled before clearing her throat.

"Ahem."
The sound startled Pastor Edwards.
"Ciara! Why didn't you knock?" the pastor asked, while pushing the money back into a basket that was on his desk.
"I'm sorry, Pastor Edwards. I did knock, but you didn't answer. That's when I opened the door," Ciara said with a smile.
"Come on in and have a seat. Make sure that door is locked behind you, sweetheart."
Ciara and Tasha briefly looked at each other.

"Who is this with you?" He spoke to Ciara, but looked at Tasha's cleavage spilling out of her dress.

"This is my sister Nina. She drove up here from Missouri with me."
She looked at Tasha for reinforcement, while holding on tightly

to her purse. The pastor didn't realize Ciara wasn't talking about Tasha. She was actually talking about the gun she had concealed in her purse.

"Oh, pleased to meet you, Nina." He reached out to shake Tasha's hand, holding it longer than necessary.

"So why did you tell me to come here when you knew your service would be finished at this time?" Ciara asked.

She grabbed his hand and placed it on the inside of her thigh.

"Is that door locked?" Pastor Edwards asked, as he removed his reading glasses.

"Everything's okay, Pastor. Now answer my question."

Tasha didn't know what was going on since this wasn't a part of their plan. "What are you doing?"

"I got everything under control, trust me. Now if we're gonna get down like this, Pastor Edwards, what's in it for us?"

"How much do you want?"

"It depends on what you want. If you want both of us, it's gonna cost you."

"I'll give you five hundred dollars," the pastor quickly replied.

"Five hundred dollars! Do we look like some prostitutes to you? This Jay Godfrey dress is more than five hundred dollars!" Ciara laughed.

Without saying a word, Pastor Edwards stood from his seat, walked towards the other side of the room, went inside his closet, and started to turn the combination lock to his safe. Ciara glanced back at Tasha. Inside, the pastor had stacks of money that filled the safe from the front all the way to the back.

"I'll give you three thousand dollars for both of you. I want to see you and your sister go at it first, though," he said, while peeling his fingers through a stack of hundred dollar bills.

Ciara grabbed the stack of money from out of the pastor's hand and threw it on the desk.

"Take your pants down," Ciara demanded.

Tasha walked over to where Ciara and Pastor Edwards were and removed his clothes. She then removed the pastor's tie and tied up his hands.

"God is good," Pastor Edwards mumbled as Ciara and Tasha began to undress, giving him a seductive strip tease show.

By the time Tasha removed her skirt, exposing her fat pussy lips, Pastor Edwards was fully erect. Ciara began licking the shaft of the pastor's penis as he put his head back and closed his eyes. That's when Ciara tapped Tasha on her leg, directing her to grab the money out of the safe. That was also when Ciara went into overdrive, giving the pastor head and allowing his dick to hit her tonsils. The sound from Ciara gagging made him want to explode in the back of her throat. Just as he was about to climax, Ciara stood up.

"What are you doing?" Pastor Edwards yelled, opening his eyes to find that Tasha had emptied the safe and now had her gun pointed directly at his head.

"Now wait one minute. Y'all don't have to do this to me," Pastor Edwards pleaded.

"We're not, you perverted motherfucker! I'm taking all your shit, and you better not say shit either."

He looked over at his empty safe and looked down at his dick with pre-cum dripping from its tip. He was naked with his hands still tied together. All he could do was curse himself now and pray for forgiveness later.

"Thanks for everything, Pastor Edwards. The community needs more people like you," Tasha said, as she grabbed the heavy bag of money.

"Don't worry, Pastor, we're not going to bother your family. This is just some insurance for us just in case you think you need to talk to the police," Ciara said, while placing the picture of the pastor's family in her bra.

Smoothly, Ciara put on her dress and blew him a kiss just before walking out of his office, as if nothing ever happened. The girls looked around to see if anyone was still at the church, but everyone was gone. They tossed the bag of money in the back of the van and drove to the highway.

"That was some crazy shit," Tasha said.

Tasha opened a bottle of water and swallowed big gulps. She held it out to Ciara in case her throat was dry after servicing the pastor.

"No, thanks. That's what his perverted ass gets! I knew he wasn't legit. He messes with women all over Gary. That's a damn shame, too, because he's ruining a lot of these young girls' lives out here."

As much as she did not want to admit it to Tasha, sucking his dick and getting away with all that money was the best adrenaline rush she'd ever experienced thus far.

"Do you think he's going to call the police?"

"No, because I have this picture right here." Ciara patted her chest.

With the picture tucked safely inside her bra, she felt relieved. Ciara knew that was all she needed to keep the pastor off of their ass.

Chapter 17

For the next couple of months, Ciara and Tasha were on a cash mission. At this point, they were robbing people and taking names later. As far as Desmond, the police ruled his death as a drug deal gone bad. The homicide detectives really didn't care because it just made their job a little easier. That's why Ciara and Tasha were able to return to Chicago so soon.

Everything was working like clockwork for the dangerous duo. They were hitting some of the major players and ballers around Chicago. They never duplicated the way they did things because they knew the streets would be talking about how they got down sooner or later. They robbed everyone that looked like they had some money, and for the perpetrators, Ciara and Tasha would just steal their cars and cheap jewelry for fun. They went from shopping at North Riverside Mall every day to taking trips to L.A. and New York. Especially Ciara; she started to buy things she couldn't even pronounce. She bought a money-green Range Rover that she kept at her townhouse located in the south suburbs of Chicago. She also had a blue face Rolex that matched her blue BMW X5. The BMW truck was her weekday car and the Range Rover was her weekend toy.

Tasha on the other hand played it cool with her money. She paid off her mother's house and bought a condo downtown with a lakefront view. She kept her same Grand Prix and painted it red. Other than Tasha's expensive taste for fashion, you really couldn't tell if she had a lot of money or not. She tried to keep a low-key profile around Chicago, but the money kept coming in too fast. Life was good for Ciara and Tasha. Almost too damn good.

******

"Okay, we have to make this quick, Tasha. I don't need any fuck-ups right now. Are you with me?"

"I'm with you. I'm just getting tired of doing this shit."

"So you're tired of getting this money?" Ciara asked, as she cocked her nickel-plated burner.

"No, I'm just tired of getting it the way we are. I mean, we have about three hundred stacks, Ciara. We can just open a business or something like that. How much money do you want?" Following Ciara's lead, Tasha loaded her gun, as well.

"How much do I want? I want it all! There's no limit to getting this money! I want all the money we can get. All the fucking money, Tasha! I lost everything and everyone, and that's not gonna happen to me again. I feel like everybody owes me. Fuck it. They do owe me. I hope you're not about to call it quits on me and we're just starting to see some real dough?"

By the look on Tasha's face, Ciara knew this would be their last heist together. She lost all the trust she had for Tasha that day. In her mind, Tasha was starting to look more like a witness to the crime instead of her partner in crime. She couldn't go down for this alone. She couldn't take another loss. Shawn and Kim were enough of a loss in Ciara's life already. She was trying to fill the emptiness in her heart with money, and she wasn't willing to allow anyone to come between the good thing she had going on.

"Enough with the soft talk. Let's go handle this business. Remember to call me and hang up when you make it to his house. Don't forget, Tasha," Ciara confirmed.

"I'm not. Let's just get it over with."

Tasha started up her Grand Prix and headed to the restaurant to meet her date, Mack.

Tasha met him at the carwash about three weeks ago, before going out of town to do a job with Ciara. Mack had an interest in Tasha right away, and it didn't take long before they drew up a plan to rob him.

Ciara knew she was dealing with a major dude, and not just some lookout boy off of the block. Mack, a well-known drug dealer in the city, and hopefully Ciara's next victim, was always on point and never let pleasure mix with his business in the streets. He was making real paper and had a fleet of vehicles, clothes, and women lined up. Women wanted to be next to him and other hustlers wanted to get at him, but Mack had too many goons on his team to let some shit like that take place. Everything seemed to be working as planned, until Mack decided to change his plans with Tasha that night.

"Sexy, I have to make a quick run before we get our night started," Mack said, as they drove in his cocaine-colored Dodge Charger on twenty-four-inch rims.

"But I thought we were going straight to your house?"

"In due time, shorty. I have to pick up some money from my worker on Sacramento."

Damn, Tasha thought. She wasn't expecting this bump in her plans but she had to roll with it. She reached into her purse and pulled out a bag of dro.

"What's that for? I don't smoke weed, and if I did, it wouldn't be any of that cheap shit. Weed slows you down, and I can't afford to slow down or lose focus, you feel me?"

Steven Morgan

Usually, when shit didn't work out as planned, the girls would go to plan B. However, since Tasha was so nervous about robbing Mack, she forgot what to do if faced with a problem like that. This wasn't feeling right tonight. Tasha needed to get away to call Ciara, but she had to wait for the right opportunity.

Mack continued to lay down the law about why he didn't do certain things, but Tasha was too nervous to listen.

Meanwhile, Ciara was sitting back smoking a blunt and listening to the Isley Brothers while waiting on Tasha and Mack to make it to the spot. She looked at the clock on her Bose car radio system and wondered what could be taking them so long. She could not wait to complete this one because she knew it was time for her to move on without Tasha, who just didn't have the same hungry spirit as she once did when they first met in jail.

Ciara took a hit of the potent bud again. Her weed man must have given her some good stuff this time, because she choked every time she took a hit of the blunt.

Back in the car, Tasha was confused on what was going on. She knew Mack didn't have a lot of money on him. Desmond use to always tell her that smart hustlers never keep a lot of money on them. Real hustlers know that at any given time they might get stuck up by a goon or harassed by the cops. Mack wasn't your normal hustler. He was very detailed with his work, and his drug operation was flawless.

Mack heard about the robberies that were going on in the hood by two females, but he wasn't sure if Tasha was one of the women involved because Ciara and Tasha never left a trace when they did jobs. The girls were very meticulous. They made every robbery seem as if the person dating the D-boy at the time was getting robbed, as well. But Mack wasn't sure until Tasha questioned why they weren't going straight to his house. This small mistake would lead to bigger problems for Tasha.

Mack had a gut feeling that he was being set up, so he took it on as a challenge. It wasn't anything new to him because people in the hood knew he had money, but they couldn't get close to him. Mack didn't allow for anyone to be with him while he was making a run, unless it was one of his workers. He didn't know Tasha at all, so he was definitely playing it safe with her.

Mack slowly pulled up to one of his trap houses near the downtown area on Division Street. He grabbed his cell phone from his lap and dialed a number. Tasha was so nervous he could see the fear in her face. Mack knew she wasn't nervous about being in the hood because he knew her type, wild and ghetto as hell. He knew stopping at his trap house would delay any plans Tasha might have had for robbing him. Mack set his opened phone on the dashboard.

"Wait right here, sexy. I'll be right back," he said, while grabbing a package from under Tasha's seat.

She watched him walk across the street towards the trap house. Everything about him screamed "major league player", from his fresh cream-colored Miskeen outfit to the slight limp in his walk and cool demeanor.

As soon as he made it inside, she pulled out her cell phone and dialed Ciara's number.

"Here this bitch is right here," Ciara said, as she answered.

"Hey, we have to change plans. I think Mack knows something is up, and I'm scared as hell. We just stopped at one of his houses and he left me in the car," Tasha nervously said, as she continued to look at the house he had gone in to make sure he wasn't coming.

"What? You scared?" Ciara paused for a second because she

could hear the fear in Tasha's voice. "Okay, let's just go with our next plan!"

"No, I don't want to rob him at all, Ciara. I think he knows I'm setting him up! He's just too smart not to know what's going on."

"Tasha, don't do this right now. This might be our biggest come up. I know you're scared, but it's too late now because the game has already started. You have to trust me on this one."

I can't believe this selfish bitch, Tasha thought. "Fuck you, Ciara!" she screamed before hanging up on her.

"I knew it," Mack mumbled. He was listening to Tasha's conversation on the house phone.

Mack was undeniably smart; he left his cell phone on because he knew Tasha would call someone as soon as he got out of the car. When he was in the car, Mack dialed the trap house's phone number and allowed it to ring until he was able to go inside and answer it.

"Man, go and put one in that bitch's head right now, Carlos!" Mack demanded, as he handed his young worker a .38 snub nose that had duct tape around the handle.

Tasha's cell phone began to vibrate.

"What do you want, Ciara? I'm not doing this shit. It's over!"

"I don't give a fuck about what you're talking about, Tasha. We're doing this tonight! I'm already here waiting for you!"

"Wait! I'm going to call you back. Someone just came out of the house."

"Call me back!" Ciara tried to yell as Tasha ended the call.

The short man walking towards the car was wearing a black hoodie with black gloves.

Tasha couldn't tell if the man was Hispanic or black because it was so dark outside.

"Hey, Mack said come inside for a minute," the man said from outside of the car window.

Tasha was scared, but she didn't want the man to know because it would be a dead giveaway. So, she slowly stepped out of the car. As she walked around the car, a cold feeling suddenly went through her body.

"Oh yeah, Mack told me to give you this, too."
"What are you talking about?" Tasha curiously asked.
The man turned around and shot Tasha two times in the chest.

The sound from the snub-nose pistol could be heard throughout the quiet city block. The impact from the two shots threw Tasha back into the street from the sidewalk. The man watched as her body hit the pavement, and then he darted through a nearby front yard. Tasha was on the ground shaking and breathing heavily. Her chest felt numb, and she could hear footsteps walking towards her. Everything else was quiet. She could only hear the footsteps and her heart beating hastily.

"Someone call the police!" Mack shouted as he stood over her body with a grin on his face.

Tasha wasn't certain if it was Mack standing above her, but she felt it had to be him because of the raspy voice she heard.
Mack didn't do anything but stare at Tasha as she gasped for air. About five minutes later, the ambulance arrived.
"Back up! I need everyone to back up!" a police officer said to the crowd of people that surrounded Tasha.
"Trick, if you live and snitch on me, I'm going to make sure you and your family are buried next to each other. Don't worry about the funeral expenses either. I'll pay for them, too, bitch," Mack whispered in Tasha's ear as the medics placed her into the back of the ambulance.
"Excuse me, sir," the paramedic said to Mack, as he tried to

maneuver Tasha inside the ambulance.

"Be careful with my neighbor," Mack lightheartedly said.

"Don't worry. We have everything under control, sir," the paramedic with dark curly hair replied.

Mack unarmed the alarm on his Charger and got inside just as the ambulance pulled off from the scene.

Tasha didn't know what was going on. Everything and everyone seemed to be going in slow motion as she felt her body draw weaker from the critical gunshot wounds. All she could do was close her eyes as the ambulance sped to the hospital.

Later on that night, Ciara made it back to her hotel room.

"I should go and kill that scary-ass bitch!" Ciara screamed as she fell back onto the bed. "Fuck, I can just go and shoot myself because I'm so pissed off! I should have seen this coming. Tasha gave me too many signs that she didn't want to live this life anymore, but I was too blind to see it."

Ciara grabbed the remote and powered on the TV. She scanned through a couple of channels before stopping on the news.

"We have just received a report that a woman has been shot in an attempted carjacking on the Westside of Chicago," the reporter stated, standing outside of the house where Tasha was shot.

"What?" Ciara sat up in the bed and turned up the volume. "Shit, I know that's Tasha. I can just feel it."

She grabbed her phone and quickly called Tasha's mother to find out if it was Tasha or not. Tasha's mother answered the phone hysterical.

"Hi, Ms. Mays. It's Ciara. Is Tasha home?"

Ms. Mays could barely answer her. "No, baby. The police just called and said Tasha was shot during a carjacking attempt!"

"Is she okay?"

"I don't know, but I'm on my way to Mount Sinai Hospital right now to see her," Ms. Mays cried.

Ciara closed her eyes and prayed to God that Tasha would be fine. She couldn't stand to lose another person.

"Okay, I'll meet you there, Ms. Mays."

Ciara felt guilty and didn't want to bother Tasha that night. She felt it would be best if she went to visit her in the morning when everything calmed down.

She turned the TV off and grabbed a pillow, squeezing it close to her chest as she thought about Tasha until she fell asleep.

The next morning, Ciara showed up to the hospital bright and early with fresh flowers, balloons, and a heavy heart. If she couldn't walk into that room by her own strength, then for Tasha's sake, she was going to have to walk in there with her head held high.

Tasha's eyes were closed and she was hooked up to four different machines. Ciara stared down at Tasha's face, hoping to be able to see her up and about enjoying life once again. She held a tight grip on Tasha's hand. A soft sob escaped Ciara's mouth as she stood there in shock.

"It's okay, Ciara. It's not your fault," Tasha whispered, as she struggled to open her weak eyelids. "I just want to be alone."

Ciara thought her girl was asleep and couldn't hear her, but Tasha heard her as soon as she stepped into the room. Tasha turned her head towards the window and stared at the small red robin that was on the windowpane.

"Don't talk. You need to rest. I really didn't mean to bother you. I just wanted to see how you were doing," Ciara softly said, while adjusting the covers on top of her.

Steven Morgan

"Take those flowers with you when you leave," Tasha said with a quivering voice, "because this is not a flower type of moment for me."
"What the hell does that mean?"
"I just don't want to be bothered by anyone. Please, just leave me alone."

Ciara didn't give it a second thought as she grabbed the flowers and stormed out. On her way out of the room, she saw Ms. Mays walking towards her with a box of donuts and hot coffee.

"Where are you going, baby?" Ms. Mays asked, as Ciara pressed the button for the elevator.
"I'm coming back later on. I have to go to an appointment right now, Ms. Mays."
"Okay, baby. Be careful."

As Ms. Mays walked into Tasha's room and closed the door, Ciara placed the flowers into a nearby trashcan and stepped inside the elevator.

Ciara felt bad about Tasha's condition, but she was not about to kiss anybody's ass. She just planned on seeing her once she was released from the hospital.

Tasha remained in the hospital for about nine weeks before being released. Although, Ciara said she wasn't going to visit Tasha again, she went up to the hospital to check on her progress everyday.

"When you get out of here today, I'm going to send you to get your hair and nails done."
"My hair? What's wrong with my hair, Ciara?"

"Girl, your hair is dry as hell. You got that Celie from *The Color Purple* look going on!"
"You're so crazy," Tasha said, barely able to run her fingers through her matted hair.

When Tasha came out of the hospital in the wheelchair, Ciara had a cherry-red 300 C parked out front.

"Ciara, whose car is this?"

"It's yours." Ciara nonchalantly put the keys in Tasha's frail hand.

"You know this isn't my style. I don't need this car."

"This is the same one you were looking at when we were in Miami." Ciara was more excited about the car than Tasha.

"Thank you, but you didn't have to do this for me."

"I know, but you know how I am. Listen, I scheduled a hair appointment for you at two o'clock, and your nail appointment is right after that. Then, we can go eat and pop some bottles in your new whip."

"That's cool, but let me go home and take a real bath first."

"Yeah, I almost forgot that you need to thoroughly wash your ass," Ciara jokingly said.

******

Later that day, Ciara drove Tasha to her hair appointment.

"This is about three hundred dollars. You should be able to get whatever you want done to your hair."

"I've never been here before, but I heard it's a good place. Thank you. I really appreciate everything you're doing for me."

Ciara replied honestly, "Don't thank me. I owe you more than words can describe. I'll be back to take you to your nail appointment in a couple of hours."

Tasha walked into the salon to see two ladies standing at the front counter.

"Hi, welcome to Hair R Us. How can I help you today?" the nimble teenage girl asked.

Steven Morgan

"Hi, I have an appointment at two o'clock."
"What's your name?"
"It's Tasha, but it may be under Ciara Blackwell."
"Yes, I have it right here. Please have a seat and we'll be with you in just a minute."

As Tasha sat down, she grabbed the *Jet* magazine from the small glass table that was in front of her. All of a sudden, a voice came out of nowhere.

"Hello, I don't mean to invade your space, sweetheart, but what did you say your name was again?"

Tasha looked up and saw a thin man standing in front of her. "It's Tasha. Why do you ask?"

"I just thought I heard you say Ciara Blackwell," the man said, then started to walk away.
"I did, but excuse me. Do I know you, sir?"

"No, you don't know me, but Ciara Blackwell is like family to me."
"Really?" she said in excitement.
"Yes, I haven't seen her in a long time, and I was wondering how you knew her."
"Ciara's my best friend. You just missed her. She just dropped me off."

"I'm glad I did miss her." The man rolled his eyes and crossed his arms across his chest.

Tasha was confused by the man's actions. "Why? Is there something wrong, sir?"

"No, but Ciara Blackwell is a hot mess. I don't trust her."
"What do you mean? Who are you?"

"My name is Byron, and I've known Ciara from a long time ago. Actually, too damn long. That hoe robbed me and put this scar on my pretty face."
Byron showed Tasha the scar on his mouth that he received

when Ciara kicked him.

"I've tried everything to cover it up, and child, let me tell you, cheap make-up isn't worth shit. If it ain't Mac, it's totally whack!"

Tasha vaguely remembered Ciara telling her bits and pieces of this story when they first met in jail.

"So you're telling me that Ciara robbed you and did this to your face?"

"And to think we're family," he replied.

"Family?" Tasha confusingly replied.

"Yes, Ciara is my sister. The family disowned her trifling ass. She used and abused everyone she came across. She took our money and never repaid us a penny."

Her thoughts were scrambled in her mind. She knew what Byron was saying had to be true because of the way Ciara acted about money. She would do whatever it took to get paid.

"Well, I'm not going to harp on the past because it's over now," Byron said, as he picked a piece of lint off of his apron.

"No, I want to know what's up with her because I thought she was different. She never told me about you or anybody else."

"Well, I'm going to be doing your hair. So, we have all day to talk about Ms. Bogus Ciara."

About two hours later, Byron was finished with Tasha's hair and his false fabrications about Ciara.

"Don't tell Ciara about anything we've talked about. Matter of fact, don't even tell her that you met me today. Here's my number. Call me anytime you would like to talk." Byron handed Tasha his business card.

"Cool, I'm going to give you my number, as well."

Byron took Tasha's phone number and stored it into his Blackberry.

"I guess I'll see you in a week or so for your touch-up, Tasha?"

Steven Morgan

"No, I'm going to call you tonight so we can talk some more about Ciara."

She took a quick look at her hair in the mirror and handed him three crisp fifty-dollar bills. When she exited the salon, she noticed Ciara was across the street waiting in the parking lot. Tasha could feel her skin crawling the closer she walked towards Ciara. She thought Ciara was a real dirty hoe for treating her family the way she had. And out of all the stories they had shared over the recent months, Tasha wondered why Ciara forgot to tell her about this.

"Your hair looks real nice." Ciara took her right hand and smoothed out a couple strands of hair on Tasha's head.

"Thanks," she sarcastically replied.

"What's wrong? You don't like it?"

"It's cool. I just have a lot on my mind right now."

Ciara sensed something had happened while Tasha was in the shop.

"Anyway, are you ready to get your nails done?"

"No, actually, you can just take me home."

"But I thought we were going to hang out?" Ciara replied, as if she was a little kid asking for McDonald's.

"Maybe next time."

"Whatever, I don't know what the hell is wrong with you. I have some business I need to take care of tonight. When I finish handling my business, I'll give you your cut."

"Cut? I don't want anything to do with that shit right now, Ciara! Don't you think I've been through enough already? I just need to relax my mind."

"You don't have to do anything because I already got it planned out. All you'll be doing is collecting when I'm finished."

"Like I said, Ciara, I don't want shit. I just want to rest. Nothing more, nothing less!"

"Well, I got some dro. We just have to stop and grab a cigarillo and some water."

"No, just take me home. You can smoke that blunt by yourself after you handle your business."

Ciara didn't understand Tasha's sudden mood swing, but she hoped it had something to do with the medicine or traumatic experience. But, Tasha had one more time to get out of line with her before she put her in her place.

"Let me hurry up and get your square ass home." Ciara ceased all talking and put her Range Rover into drive.

"Whatever, I'll be a square then!" Tasha shot back, rolling her eyes as she looked out of the passenger's side window.

Ciara just looked over at her and then turned up Lil Wayne's "Lollipop" on the radio.

The ride to Tasha's condo was very tense and uncomfortable. When Ciara pulled up front, she tried to say bye, but Tasha didn't even turn around to acknowledge her. Ciara didn't wait for Tasha to make it inside before she peeled off.

"Fuck her! Fuck everybody!" Ciara screamed.

Ciara pressed her Manolo Blahnik shoe down harder on the gas pedal and blasted the radio while driving home on the congested Eisenhower expressway.

Chapter 18

Ciara's bags were packed and she had everything in order for her weekend getaway to Las Vegas. All that was left to do now was get a good night's sleep and wake up on time in the morning so she wouldn't miss her flight.

She double-checked her security system before grabbing a bottle of water from her refrigerator and heading to her bedroom. The room was quiet as Ciara pounced onto her bed, leaving a coco butter scent in the air. Getting comfortable under the Egyptian cotton sheets, she pulled the covers close to her chest. She loved to leave her window open just enough to feel the windy city breeze blow through her almond-colored blinds. It didn't take long for Ciara to fall into a deep sleep. Different emotions overtook her dreams as she saw images of Tasha being shot. The scene replayed over and over in her head as she tossed and turned in her king-size bed. The images were vivid. They hit too close to home and Ciara's reality. She could only reach out her hand as Tasha begged for help while blood poured from her body. A constant spray of bullets being released from the perpetrator's gun drowned Tasha's cries out. Ciara jumped up in her bed with sweat covering her entire body.

"What the hell is going on?" Ciara screamed loudly, turning her head from side to side, trying to adjust her eyes to the darkness in the room. She turned on the lamp that was on the nightstand and quickly dialed Tasha's number.

"Hello," Tasha reluctantly answered.

"Look, I'm sorry about the way I've been acting towards you. I've been inconsiderate about what happened to you. I don't know what I was going through. You're my girl, and I should've listened when you expressed being scared that night you got shot. I'm sorry, and I will never jeopardize losing you again."

"I don't know what to say, Ciara. I just don't know," Tasha replied, confused.

"You don't have to say anything. I had to say my peace and admit to my wrongdoings. It was my fault and I'm sorry. Hey, I want to spend my birthday with you when I get back. What do you think?"

Inside, Tasha still didn't feel that Ciara was sincere about what happened to her, and she didn't think she would ever be able to completely forgive and forget.

"Well, I have to go. I'll talk to you later."

"I'm leaving for Vegas in the morning. I'll call you when I get there and let you know how it is."

"Yeah, sure." Tasha hung up the phone before Ciara could say another word.

Ciara wanted the conversation to go different, but at least she was able to say what she needed to say. She felt better and hoped that Tasha would come around soon.

******

The pilot announcing that the plane was about to land at the McCarran International Airport awakened Ciara. She glanced around the packed airplane as she buckled her seatbelt, preparing for the landing. After touching down, she quickly grabbed her Louis Vuitton carry-on bag, exited the plane, and retrieved the rest of her luggage from baggage claim.

The dryness of the desert weather hit her when she walked outside to hail a taxi. The humidity left her soft, moisturized skin sticky and wet. Ciara jumped into the cab, enjoying the air conditioner, and asked the driver to take her to the best hotel in Vegas. The cabbie stared at her in his cracked rearview mirror and noticed her sparkling jewelry as he pulled away from the curb.

When the taxi pulled up to a light, Ciara noticed two Caucasian men getting out of a black-on-black Corvette. Both men were heavyset and sported all black.

"Stop! I want to get out right here," she screamed to the driver.

"Pay me first! You owe me twenty dollars," the foreign driver yelled, reaching for his Jackson.

"Calm down! I'm going to pay you. Y'all cab drivers are thirsty as hell." Ciara handed him a crispy one-hundred-dollar bill.

The driver examined the bill before placing it in the cash slot in the console.

"You can keep the change, too," she stated, then jumped out of the cab with her belongings.

Ciara walked into the casino and placed her bags near a plant that stood about six feet tall. The first order of business on her agenda was following those same two men to figure out if they were big-time gamblers or not. She kept a short distance behind the men as she trailed them around the casino. One of the men had a long ponytail with a face full of craters. He walked over to the roulette table and dropped down ten fifty-dollar bills. After losing that five hundred, he placed another five on the same number.

Ciara's hand began to itch. She could feel herself getting closer to gaining their money. She continued to watch the men as she tested her luck on the slot machine that was only about twenty feet away.

About two hours later, the men grabbed the remaining chips from the table and walked towards the casino's elevator. She followed the men and was able to get on the elevator just as the doors closed.

"How are you doing this evening?" one of the men asked, while staring at Ciara's ass from behind.

The liquor on his breath was strong, and Ciara was turned off by the stench.

"I'm okay. How are you gentlemen doing tonight? Have any luck on those rigged-up machines?"

"No, we had a bad night. Lady luck wasn't on our side tonight. How about you? Did you have any luck?"

"I really didn't play that much. I'm just trying to focus for my interview tomorrow," she lied.

"What interview? What is it that you do?"

"This will be my third interview this week with the Bunny Ranch on Monday. I decided to come a couple of days early so I can get rid of these butterflies."

The two men looked at one another when Ciara mentioned the Bunny Ranch.

"Are you going to be one of the working girls, or are you just going to clean up the place?"

"Do I look like a maid to you?" she asked confidently.

The two men gawked at her in the elevator as she seductively stood and waited by the door for it to open. Both men grew excited by the sight of her round ass.

The man quickly asked, "Hey, what's your name?"

"My Bunny Ranch name or my government name?" Ciara flirtatiously asked.

"Both," the man replied.

"Gorgées is my government and Bunny Ranch name."

"You are gorgeous."

"Big Papa, I didn't say gorgeous. I said Gorgées. It's French. Go and look it up."

Before the doors could close completely, the man with the ponytail stepped in front of the sensor and the doors opened wide.

"Why don't you come up to our room and have a drink. We can

drink some Martini's and talk."

"I don't know. Maybe some other time guys."

Ciara knew that a quick dick suck could get her some fast money, but she knew the two men had much more than "dick sucking money" to give. She had to come up with a plan so she could get the real dough. Ciara's slick Chicago mentality kicked in as she casually walked back towards the elevator.

"Listen to me," she demanded, speaking slow enough so the man could follow her glossy wet lips. "This is not a good time. I have a lot of business to take care of in the morning with the interview and all. After I leave the interview, though, we can hang out and do whatever."

The man knew Ciara won this round. He didn't want to force her to stay, but her sex appeal had his mind wondering. Although he knew nothing would happen tonight, the man believed he would see her again.

"After Collin and I gamble, we will be at the Ambassador Suite Hotel around eight. We can celebrate if you get hired. You'll love the Ambassador Suites. Rumor has it that The Beatles and Elvis stayed there."

"I never got your name, Big Papa."

"The name is Roy," he quickly replied. "Here's my number. Give me a call when you get out of your interview. I'll have a limo pick you up."

"Okay, I'll see you then."

Roy winked at Ciara and took a step back so the elevator door could close. Collin remained quiet but observant.

Ciara waited for the elevator door to completely close before she pressed for the elevator to go back down so she could retrieve her luggage. She stepped onto the elevator and took a deep breath as the door closed behind her. She didn't have much time to plan out her robbery attempt. The window of opportunity only presented her with less than twenty-four hours to come up with a plan that would work.

Discombobulated

******

The lobby gave Ciara a visual of her favorite green item, someone else's money. The soft green carpet coordinated well with the cream and money-green fixtures that completed the large, busy hotel lobby.

She turned around on her heels, surveying her soft yellow dress in the mirror near the elevators. The dress fitted her well. The black thong she wore under her dress allowed her ass cheeks to bounce as she walked towards the front glass doors. Her body language gave way to a hint of sexiness. Not only was she getting the attention of the men, but the women were also looking.

Ciara was walking out of the lobby's doors at the same time that her limo was pulling up. The white Chrysler 300 stretch limo pulled up in front of Ciara and a million eyes zoomed in on her.

When the chauffeur jumped out to open the door, Ciara's confidence went into overdrive from all of the attention she was receiving as she stepped into her next money scheme. The plush leather formed to Ciara's body like it was programmed to do so. She could smell the fresh leather in the air as she grabbed a bottle of champagne that was already placed in a bronze-colored bucket of chipped ice. She didn't bother to grab one of the elegant champagne flutes. Instead, she blessed the champagne by tapping it twice with her hand and drank directly from the mouth of the bottle. This was a ritual that Ciara and Kim would do when they were teenagers.

Tonight, she wasn't just celebrating for herself. She felt good on the inside and looked even better on the outside. It was the same feeling that Shawn once gave her when they were happy and in love. Life hadn't felt this way in a long time.

Ciara stretched out on the leather seats and closed her eyes, while sipping the chilled champagne until the limo cruised to its destination.

Twenty-five minutes later, the limo arrived at the Ambassador Suites Hotel. Ciara placed the uncorked bottle of champagne back into the bucket of ice, looked at her appearance in the mirror, waited for the driver to open the door, and then stepped out, placing one heel on the concrete at a time. It was fifty people outside taking pictures with their camera phones and other recording devices.

"Miss, Roy wanted me to inform you that he will be in Room 417 waiting for your arrival," the young chauffeur politely said. Ciara reached into her purse, pulling out a crisp twenty-dollar bill for the driver. He gladly accepted the tip, placed it in his front jacket pocket, and prepared to go to his next destination. Walking into the hotel, she noticed an attractive man, who was easy on the eyes, standing behind the desk.

"Welcome to the Ambassador Suites Luxury Hotel. My name is Scott. How may I help you this lovely evening?"

"Will you call Room 417 and tell Roy that his friend has arrived? Please and thank you!"

"No problem. May I give him your name?"

"Ciara."

She took a few steps away from the desk and looked around the hotel as the clerk called up to Roy's room.

"Ma'am, Mr. Ellsworth said you may come up to his suite."

"Thank you," she replied.

Ciara took the elevator to the fourth floor. When she stepped off, Roy was already there waiting for her.

"Damn, you scared the shit out of me, Roy," Ciara yelped, as she braced herself against the wall."

"I'm sorry, sweetheart. I was just about to come and get you. How are you? How was the interview?"

"Everything is alright, I guess. I didn't do so well on the interview," Ciara lied.

"What happened? Did you shit your skirt?" Roy joked.

"I rather not talk about it."

"Oh, lighten up. You win some and you lose some."

As they walked into the room, the scent of Chinese food hit Ciara's nostrils immediately. The spacious, old fashion suite was beautiful. She walked through the luxury suite admiring the ambiance of the room.

"Look at the Jacuzzi," Collin yelled, as he walked over towards her wearing nothing but a bathrobe. "It's in the middle of the damn floor."

Ciara continued her tour and came across a table that had stacks of money on top of it. The two men didn't say anything to her as she stood by the table.

"How much did you win today, Roy?"

"Nothing. I didn't even get a chance to gamble. That's my money to go home with."

"So you're telling me that you're going to take all of this to your wife?"

She waited on her answer, but Roy never responded.

"Do you want something to drink, Ciara?"

"How do you know my name is Ciara?"

"Did I say Ciara? I meant Gorgées," Roy said in a high-pitched voice.

She ignored Roy because she knew she slipped up by giving the clerk her real name earlier.

Roy grabbed three glasses from the bar and poured the fine-tasting Hardy Cognac his money could buy. Ciara watched his every move as he prepared the mellow drinks for the three of them, but her mind and eyes continued to glance back at the stacks of money on the table.

"I'll be back," Collin informed them. Then, he went into another room in the suite.

Roy grabbed his drink and took a seat next to Ciara on the couch that was near the Jacuzzi. She took a sip of her smooth drink, while he watched her. He lit his cigar and held it out for her, but she declined. Collin walked back into the room and dropped a small green bag on the table. Ciara looked at the bag, then at Roy, and finally at Collin.

"I don't know if she plays this type of game, Collin? I'm not sure if she's a big girl."

Ciara stood up from couch with a perplexed look on her face.

"What the hell is going on here? What is in that damn bag?"

Collin flopped down on the chair across from Ciara and Roy.

"Have a seat, sweetheart. This isn't what you think it is," Roy said.

A small Reynolds wrapped package fell from the green bag.

"What the hell is that?" she anxiously asked.

"It's some Chinese tobacco," Collin answered. "This shit is what makes their eyes squint."

Roy removed the tightly wrapped plastic off of the package. The pungent smell was unbelievable and offensive; it caused Ciara's eyes to water.

"I don't know what that is, but I know it's definitely not my type of party," she said, covering her nose with her hand.

Roy asked, "Do you smoke pot?"

Ciara remained quiet.

Collin grabbed the bag so he could smoke the Chinese opium tobacco. Roy joined in on the festivities. Ciara watched intently as the men took turns enjoying the drug. It didn't take long before the two men began to feel the effects.

"I love the look on a person's face right before you kill them," Collin mumbled.

"I don't like any of it. I just like it when we get paid," Roy retorted.

"What are y'all talking about? What do y'all do for a living?" Ciara asked the question, but wasn't sure if she was prepared for the answer.

"We work for a very important person in Florida. He pays us well for our services."

"What services might that be?"
Both men ignored her question. She stared at the men and saw Roy's eyes were glossy and dark red from the drug. Collin was just as high. Both men were in their own lifted world. Ciara looked over to see if the money was still on the table. Maybe this was her chance to grab it and leave.
When Ciara turned back to face the men again, Collin was standing right there in her personal space.
"Bang! Bang!" Collin playfully yelled, as he imitated holding a gun in his hand, pointing it in Ciara's face.
"Oh my God! What the hell is wrong with you?" she screamed. Collin held his empty glass in the air, hoping he had some cognac left to finish off.
"It's nothing left in that damn glass, Collin! You've been swallowing down liquor like it's water. That man can drink anybody you know under the table."
"I want to know what type of services you and Collin provide for the important man down in Florida. I mean, are y'all hitmen or drug dealers? So you're not going to tell me, Roy?"
"Just tell her," Collin urged, then left the two alone to go into the bathroom.
"You haven't even told us what Gorgées stands for."
Without warning, Ciara dropped to her knees in front of Roy and unbuckled his pants. He didn't resist her actions. Just her touch alone had him fully erect. She softly wrapped her hand around his penis and stroked it up and down.
"Gorgées means swallow in French. Is that what you want me to do?"
Roy was speechless. He let out a rough moan as Ciara placed his dick into her mouth. It didn't take much for her to please him. The combination of drugs, liquor, and Ciara's head game had him at his breaking point. With every lick of Roy's shaft, his moans became louder and deeper.
"Do you want me to swallow, daddy?"

"Yes, baby. Don't stop," Roy begged.

"Are you going to tell me what you do for a living? Or do I have to suck it out of you, daddy?"

Ciara worked her full lips down his shaft, along the thick vein, and to his balls.

"I'm an enforcer. I do jobs for my boss and get paid. That's all. Keep going, baby."

For the moment, Ciara didn't want to rob the men, but her greed told her something different as she continued to service him.

"Let's go in the other room," she demanded, while standing up and undressing.

Roy was in a daze as he stared at Ciara's nicely trimmed pussy in front of him. Her nipples were hard as concrete, and her ass bounced in front of him as she walked away. Collin walked out of the bathroom interrupting their game.

"What do we have here?" Collin asked.

Ciara signaled for Collin to join them, and he immediately removed his bathrobe, exposing his hairy Italian body. One had the smallest dick and the other had more hair on his body than she had ever witnessed.

After they made it into the bedroom, Ciara got on all fours on top of the bed.

"Come and get it, if you want it," she said, licking her finger and rubbing her clitoris.

Collin began to stroke himself, and Roy walked over to Ciara. Roy slapped her ass and laughed.

"I always wanted to do that to a black woman's ass. Baby got back!"

Ciara was a great actress. If only the men knew that she was grossed out beyond belief. She wanted to vomit with his every touch, but the thought of the money kept her in the game. She just wanted all of it to be over.

Roy entered her from the back, placed one hand on Ciara's butt, and began to pump. He wasn't working with much, so his

Discombobulated

pumps were short and fast. She pretended to be pleased, moaning loudly to cover up her disgust. Sweat dripped from Roy's face onto Ciara's ass, and she thought she was going to lose her composure and run out of the room yelling.

Collin was now standing at attention, as he walked over to Ciara and placed his dick in her face. She tried to ignore his advances. She already sucked one dick and was not in the mood to suck his tiny, hairy one.

"Come here," Ciara instructed, as she stopped Roy and signaled for Collin to get his turn.

Roy didn't care; he was still trying to catch his breath. Ciara rolled over onto her back and opened her legs as wide as they could go. She gave a new definition to the term spread eagle. Collin placed his head in between Ciara's legs and began licking her clit. She felt a tingle in her spine when his warm lips touched her pussy. He licked her as if he was tongue kissing it. Ciara didn't expect Collin to handle his business like this. She was ready to explode in his mouth.

Just then, Collin stopped and slid his dick inside her. His technique was strange. He was sort of rough, and it seemed as if he didn't know what he was doing. Although she accepted this quest, she was starting to feel violated. His hairy chest and arms felt like sandpaper against her soft skin. As she prayed for him to finish quickly, Collin pulled out and ejaculated on Ciara's leg. He was in her raw the entire time.

"I'm not finish yet," Roy said.

"Okay, lay down. I'm about to take care of you, daddy. Turn on some music so we can heighten the mood."

Following her directions, Roy turned on the radio. Collin grabbed a towel that was lying on the floor and left the room.

"Just relax, daddy. I'm going to take care of you. Let me go and grab some lotion out of my bag."

Ciara couldn't go another round with the men. She had to figure out a way to get the money, exit the room, and leave the hotel.

When Ciara heard Collin turn on the shower, she ran over to the couch by the Jacuzzi and quickly got dressed. She quietly walked towards the room to see if Roy was still lying down. She looked into the room and was relieved to see Roy was sound asleep with the music playing. This was the best chance she had, so she had to act fast. As Ciara walked towards the table full of money, Collin came from out of the bathroom.
"What the hell are you doing?" Collin screamed, as Ciara quickly gathered the money. "Roy, come here!"
She snatched two bundles of the money and tried to run past Collin, but they both tumbled to the floor when he tried to grab her.
"Get the fuck off of me," Ciara screamed. Collin's grasp on her was frightening.
"Calm down, you whore. You tried to rob us." Collin slapped Ciara with a closed fist.
Roy was in a deep sleep, and the radio was playing too loudly for him to hear what was going on inside of the suite. Ciara struggled to escape. Collin lost his footing and they both fell again. This time, he hit his head on the edge of the table. His grip became weaker and Ciara jumped up. She heard a sound coming from the other room, and she responded swiftly by getting up, running out of the room, and leaving the two men and the money behind.
They're going to kill me. I have to get out of Vegas, Ciara thought, as she ran to safety. When she made it to the lobby, she spotted the attractive man from earlier.
"Please help me! These two guys tried to rape me! Please help me!" Ciara shouted, grabbing the man's arm and sobbing.
The man looked at the large hand print on her face.
"Okay, calm down. Do you want to call the police?"
"No! Just take me to the fucking airport!"
The attractive man agreed and escorted Ciara to his van that was outside of the Ambassador. During the drive to the airport, she

Discombobulated

went over the incident in her head. Two men. Money. Unsafe
sex. Hitmen. No money. Death. She was about to go crazy
before she even had a chance to catch a plane out of Las Vegas.
The driver reached the airport in no time at all. Ciara pulled out
a large bill from her wallet and gave it to the man.
"Thank you for taking me to the airport. Here's your money.
Please don't tell anyone you brought me to the airport. I fear for
my safety, and I don't want them to come looking for me."
"I don't want your money, ma'am. I just hope you're safe and
that you seek some medical attention when you get to wherever
it is you're going. Are you sure you don't want to call the
police?"
"I'm sure."
Ciara made sure she had all of her belongings. She didn't want
to leave behind any information about herself in Vegas. Then
she just turned away and left the man standing there.

chapter 19

It took Ciara a couple of days to recuperate from her experience in Las Vegas. During her entire recovery period, she watched re-runs of *Friends* and *Martin*. Her repeated calls to Tasha were ignored, and she didn't even feel like shopping for an outfit for her birthday that was days away. The cold and gloomy Chicago weather sure wasn't a good way to add cheer to her situation. After finishing off her second bottle of Nuvo, Ciara walked into the bathroom, with the marble floor cold underneath her feet, to relax in her awaiting hot bath water.

She slowly undressed in front of the mirror and felt disgusted by what she saw. Her image was still as beautiful as the Chicago skyline, but she felt ashamed of the person she had become. Ciara walked into her bedroom, turned on the radio that was mounted on the wall above her vanity, set the disc to track four, and left the room. As she walked into the kitchen, her phone began to ring. She knew Tasha could be calling her back, but she wasn't going to let anyone ruin her mood. Continuing on with her peaceful night, Ciara grabbed a champagne flute out of her cabinet and placed it on the granite countertop. She reached into the freezer and pulled out another bottle of Nuvo. The cold bottle in her hand made her nipples erect. She poured the Nuvo into the glass and carried it back into the bathroom. Carefully, she stepped into the hot bath water, testing the temperature with her toes. After placing the glass of Nuvo on the edge of the tub, she submerged her entire body into the water until she adjusted to the temperature. Ciara closed her eyes as she sipped her Nuvo, repeating Ron Isley's lyrics.

Suddenly, she was overcome with emotions. She missed Kim. She felt stupid for allowing a strange man to hit it raw, and she was missing the touch from her deceased, estranged husband. Instead of feeling sad while thinking about Shawn, she got horny. Ciara took another sip of her drink and placed the glass on the floor next to the tub. Gently, she rubbed her breast and opened her legs, then closed them tightly to feel the pressure from her thighs squeezing together. She continued to rub all over her body until the sensation from her touch made her quiver. Ciara placed her right leg onto the edge of the tub and fondled her wet pussy lips. She was in need of a strong, powerful climax. The feeling from the orgasm made her body tremor and her eyes flutter. Her body felt weak, but relaxed. The feeling didn't last too long, though, because her phone began to ring again just as she was about to take another sip of her drink.

She grabbed a towel from her closet and went to answer it.

"Hello!"

"It's about time! Why haven't you been answering your phone? I thought something was wrong."

"Tasha, I've been calling you for two days and you never answered. So don't give me that shit about why I wasn't answering my phone. Where the hell have you been is the question."

"You're right, girl. I'm tripping. I've been busy. I just enrolled in school at Malcolm X College. I'm trying to do some different shit. I need to get my life together. You should go up there and enroll, too. Have you ever thought about that?" Tasha asked.

"School? No, thank you, boo! I have bigger fish to fry. Besides, my birthday is in two days. I'm not trying to be sitting in anybody's classroom on my birthday."

"Damn, you're getting old," Tasha joked. "That's why I was calling you. I want to take you to New York for your birthday. We can shop and go out, or do whatever. It's going to be a ball. Are you up for that?"

"Well, I guess that'll be cool. When did you want to leave?"

"We can leave the day before your birthday so we can start celebrating early. If not, we can just leave on your birthday. It's up to you."

"Okay, that's fine. I'm going to get my things together, and we can leave in the morning once we're packed."

"Good! I'll call you in then," Tasha replied, then hung up.

******

Tasha and Ciara chatted the whole duration of the plane ride to New York City. Tasha wasn't use to flying, so she needed constant conversation and an unlimited supply of liquor during the first-class flight to calm her nerves.

The day had started off without a hitch. The ladies enjoyed a turbulent-free plane ride, quick retrieval of their luggage, and a bumpy, noisy cab ride to the hotel.

The taxi driver dropped them off in front of the historic 5th Avenue Club hotel. Ciara looked up at the fifty-floor building and couldn't believe how beautiful it was. She loved everything about New York and the traffic on 51st Avenue added to the excitement and energy. The ladies checked into the room and rushed upstairs to relax.

"Tasha, this hotel is the shit. I can't believe you did all of this for me," Ciara said, as she bounced on the large pillow top mattress. "This is the best birthday I can remember, and we're just getting started. I know a rapper or somebody important must be staying here tonight."

"This room is so beautiful. I might decide to make another trip back here for my birthday. It's a little expensive, but I think it's

worth it. Where did you want to go for dinner?"
"We can order room service and party like rock stars right here."
Tasha neatly placed her bags on the floor and called to order food. After ordering two steak dinners, she grabbed two bottles of champagne out of her luggage and handed them to Ciara.
"What's this?"
"It's champagne, Ciara. Duh!"
"I know that much, but what kind is it?"
"That's 1995 Krug Clos Ambonnay Champagne. It's better than Moet and Dom P."
"Well, it looks cheap as hell. Better than Moet and Dom P? Please, this looks like it's straight from the dollar store," Ciara teased.
Tasha had to laugh. "Trust me when I say that shit wasn't cheap. Girl, that's seven thousand dollars you're holding right there. It was thirty-five hundred for each bottle."
"I know you didn't pay seven thousand dollars for this champagne?" Ciara screamed.
"It's nothing. You only turn thirty once. I felt it was worth it. Besides, you bought me a car, and that was well over thirty grand."
"First of all, I'm not thirty. Thank you very much. I'm only twenty-something years old. Don't you forget that! I'm just saying that you didn't have to do this for me. I'm just happy that I didn't have to spend my birthday alone."
"Twenty-something, huh? Whatever you say. Just pop open one of those bottles so I can get my drink on."
Ciara poured Tasha and herself a glass of Ambonnay champagne before she went into her purse and pulled out a bag of weed that was hidden down in a bag of Cheetos. The strong marijuana scent had overpowered both the Cheetos and cucumber melon body lotion she had in her purse. How she got it past security was baffling.

Ciara rolled the first blunt, while Tasha finished her second glass. Ciara handed the blunt to her and tossed the bag of weed on the nightstand next to the bed. The expensive champagne and Kush weed would surely put them on another level.

Soon enough, the weed and alcohol had things going in another direction. They rapped along to Snoop Dog's "Gin and Juice", while seeing if one could jump up higher on the bed than the other. After the fake Snoop concert, they had a dance competition. Ciara wasn't much of a dancer, so she just sat back as Tasha performed in front of her. Tasha rolled and twisted around the room giving Ciara a show and even a lap dance. They were in their own little world until they heard two knocks at the door. Tasha smiled at Ciara and went to answer it. Two men in suits stood on the other side of the threshold waiting to be let in.

"Tasha, is there something you should be telling me?" Ciara asked, as the men stood in front of her.

"Quiet! We have some questions to ask you, Mrs. Blackwell. Do you know what time it is?" the man asked Ciara.

Before she could answer, the men snatched off their clothes and began their dance routine. The well-built strippers surrounded Ciara as she sat on the edge of the bed gasping for air and rubbing her hands across the stripper's washboard abs.

Tasha wanted Ciara to have a little fun alone, so she excused herself and went into the bathroom to freshen up and change clothes. When she came back out, Tasha was wearing a Wicked Temptations floral bra and panty set. Her double D breasts could barely fit into the cups of the bra. She joined the men and continued her sexy dance for Ciara.

Ciara watched Tasha as she dipped to the floor and came back up between her legs. It took a lot of self-control for her not to caress Tasha's body. She always felt that Tasha was attractive, but this time, she wanted to taste her. Then suddenly, Tasha stood up and walked into the bathroom.

"What's wrong?" Ciara asked, following behind her friend.
"I'm not feeling good. I don't know if it was the food or the champagne, but I have to relax for a moment."
"Okay, I'm going to tell them to go."
"No, wait! I'll be fine. I just need to shake this queasy feeling. It's your birthday, and I don't want you to stop enjoying yourself because I can't hold my alcohol."
Ciara shrugged her shoulders and snickered. "I'm cool. I didn't like their stiff-ass dancing anyway."
Ciara escorted the strippers out of the room so that Tasha could lie down and sleep. As she sat and watched Tasha snoring softly, something came over her. Ciara crawled under the covers next to Tasha. She couldn't resist.
"What are you doing?" Tasha asked in a raspy voice.
Ciara kissed on Tasha's body and removed Tasha's panties with her mouth like a groom removing the garter off his bride at a wedding reception. Tasha did not protest or put up a fight; she surrendered to Ciara's passion. Ciara softly kissed around Tasha's clit and slid two of her fingers into her pussy. The in-and-out movement of Ciara's fingers felt almost as good as a man's dick to Tasha. On this night, the two friends became two curious freaks.
Tasha reached over and grabbed the blunt that was in the ashtray by the bed and lit it. Ciara pushed Tasha's legs back, almost behind her head, continuously licking and sucking on her pussy lips and clit. Tasha's moaning became louder. Ciara didn't let up either. The louder the moans, the faster Ciara's tongue went. This was a feeling Tasha had never felt before. Not even Desmond gave her such satisfaction.
Wanting Ciara to experience what she was feeling, she told her, "Get up. Let me show you something. I bet you have never seen this before."
Tasha took the blunt out of her mouth and placed the unlit end between her pussy lips. Tasha's pussy started moving like it was

throbbing and smoke began to surface. She then laid Ciara back on the bed and aggressively ate her out. The rough oral sex made Ciara have back-to-back orgasms.

The night would only get better as the party moved to the shower. There, Ciara poured champagne down Tasha's body, trying to catch every drop in her mouth. After their three hours of excitement, they fell asleep on the floor by the foot of the bed, drunk and naked.

The next morning, Ciara woke up and Tasha was gone. She figured Tasha was out shopping or getting breakfast. She walked through the room towards the bathroom and noticed the room was spotless. The champagne bottles weren't on the floor and her clothes were neatly folded on the bathroom sink. Tasha's bags were gone.

Ciara grabbed her phone from her purse and dialed Tasha's number, but the call went straight to voicemail. Her left eye caught a white piece of paper with what looked like Tasha's writing scribbled across the front.

Ciara,

I don't know how to feel about what happened last night. I don't know if I should feel stupid or embarrassed. Your scheme to get me drunk and vulnerable was selfish. I guess you always get what you want at the end. It's all about, Ciara, huh? On the flipside of this, I'm not blaming you for everything. I'm aware of my actions, as well. My life has gone downhill since I've met you. That robbing and lesbian shit is for the birds. I will leave that lifestyle for you. Don't count me in anymore. Thanks for nothing.

Tasha

P.S. Find your own way back to Chicago

Chapter 20

Tasha frequently pondered over the night she got shot and the incident in New York with Ciara. She kept replaying both of the scenes in her head. She looked in the mirror, which she seemed to do quite often these days. The thick, ugly scars on her chest were permanent reminders of how God spared her life and permitted her to live another day.

She never forgave Ciara for making her go through with the plan to rob Mack that night. She knew it wasn't safe, but Ciara urged her to continue with Plan B. Tasha knew she was to blame just as much as Ciara. She should have never asked her to rob Desmond. That was the catalyst that set the other robberies in motion. It seemed as if everything Byron said about Ciara was true.

Tasha grabbed her phone and dialed Byron's number.

"Hey, Byron, I know it's late, but I can't get any sleep."

"It's cool, but what's wrong?" Byron asked, as he lowered the sound on his television.

"I can't sleep. I keep thinking about Ciara."

"Why do you keep thinking about that hussy?"

Tasha took a deep breath. "Please don't judge me, but I've done a lot of bad things in my past. Ciara and I use to set men up and rob them. We only robbed drug dealers or people who we thought had money. I guess I'm to blame for the whole thing because it was my idea to rob my ex-boyfriend first. That was a big mistake because he died during our robbery attempt. From that point on, it's like Ciara became addicted to robbing and getting fast money. It was an ugly game we played, and it got even uglier when I got shot."

"Wait a minute, Tasha. You were shot?" Byron asked, while turning up the volume on his cell phone.

"I was shot twice in the chest at close range. A drug dealer named Mack had one of his workers shoot me. I'm sorry for calling and bothering you like this, but I felt so connected with you when you told me about your situation with her. I felt so relieved when I knew someone else shared the same pain as me. The only way I can have peace is if I pay Ciara back in some kind of way. I'm totally wrong for feeling this way, but I want my revenge, Byron."

"Now calm down. I know you want to get payback, but you have to be smart about it. You don't want anything wrong to happen and that bitch accidentally dies, do you?"

"At this point, I don't care what happens to her," she angrily answered.

Byron could hear the hurt in Tasha's voice. "Okay, meet me tomorrow at the salon around six. We can come up with something to put this bitch out of her misery. By the way, Tasha, I'm going to bring someone else who can help us out with this."

"That's cool. Thank you so much for allowing me to vent."

"It's okay. We all have to do it sometime. Just try and get some sleep, girl."

As soon as Tasha hung up, Byron called Decorey.

"You wouldn't believe this shit. I got some news about someone from our past."

"What are you talking about, Byron?"

"I know someone who knows Ciara Blackwell," he confidently said.

"Yeah, right," Decorey replied.

"I'm so serious, and I think it's time we paid this bitch back for good."

Decorey and Byron had been yearning for another chance to see Ciara again.

"Who is this person that knows Ciara?"

"A young girl who came to the shop to get her hair done said she's been hanging with Ciara for quite some time now. She told me everything about that bitch. How they use to rob drug dealers and everything."

"Let's see if we can use the girl you met to get us to that cunt."

"I'm going to fuck her up, too! I haven't been doing all this Tae-Bo shit for nothing, Decorey."

"Calm down. I'll just see you later on today. We can talk about everything then."

"Okay, later."

******

The next morning after Ciara made it back from New York, she called Tasha.

"Hello, who is this?" Tasha answered, still asleep.

"Are you still in the bed?"

"Yeah, what time is it and who is this?"

"It's about ten o'clock, and you need to be up and ready to get out."

Tasha finally caught on to whom the voice belonged to on the other end.

"What do you want, Ciara?"

Steven Morgan

"Well, I didn't want to bother you. I just wanted to let you know that I'm going out of town tonight."

"Okay, and why are you telling me this?" Tasha asked, while rolling over in her bed with her eyes still closed.

"Wait a minute. You haven't been acting the same. It's like you did a three hundred and sixty degree turn on me. What's wrong? Did I do something to you? What happened in New York was mutual. I didn't force you to do anything that you didn't want to do. The fucked up part about it is that you left me in New York. You couldn't even talk to me like a grown woman. Now that was some crazy shit."

"No, I just haven't been in the mood lately, and I have a lot on my mind. I felt embarrassed about what happened between us. I'm not a lesbian, Ciara. I just don't know what to say."

"Well, you need to take a page out of my book of life called "Fuck It and Smoke a Blunt". We can't change what happened between us."

Those comments made Tasha open her eyes completely.

"See, that's your fucking problem. You don't have any control of yourself. All you do is smoke and fucking think of ways to rob somebody. And I'm tired of your shit, Ciara! You fucking seduced me bitch!"

Ciara had to take a quick look at her phone.

"First of all, who the fuck do you think you're talking to? Second, bitch, you can't judge me because you ain't me. I do what I please because I'm a grown-ass woman. I have to smoke and live stress-free. Have you ever lost your husband and best friend in the same day? No, you haven't. So, don't fucking tell me shit! You still got this chip on your shoulder from when you got shot. I really think you blame me for that shit! But let's get it straight and out on the table, Tasha. You're the one who introduced me to this shit! It's a part of the game, and you should know that. This is the life we both decided to live. Now something happens to you and you want to have a change of heart! If it were me who got shot, would you even give a damn? Smoking blunts out of your pussy. I guess I made you do that shit, too, huh?"

"Hello! Hello!" Ciara hadn't even realized Tasha hung up on her.   "5…4…3…2…1…" Ciara started counting so she could calm down before she lost it.

******

Later on that day, Tasha met Byron at the salon.

"Hey, Byron, how are you?" she asked, snacking on a bag of Doritos in her hand.

"I'm doing well. I would like you to meet my brother, Decorey. Decorey, this is Tasha, my good friend."

"Nice to meet you, Tasha," Decorey replied, shaking Tasha's hand.

"Are you ready to get down to business, Tasha?" Byron asked.

"Of course, but is it safe to talk here?" she asked, while looking around the fully staffed salon.

"We can go in the back and talk things over there," Byron suggested. "I'm about to step into the back for a second. If any of my clients come in, tell them that I will be with them shortly," he instructed his co-workers.

"First things first, Tasha, I don't know what kind of beef you have with Ciara, but honestly, I don't care. I owe her for the bullshit that she put us through," Decorey said, glancing over at Byron sitting at the desk.

"Even if I have to take matters into my own hands, I'm going to make sure she pays for what she has done. You understand me?"

Tasha nodded her head.

"This is the deal, Tasha. As you know, we have a past with Ciara, and our last encounter with her didn't end too well. I know for a fact that if you tell her that you know us, she would be interested in finding out more about our whereabouts. Byron told me about how you and Ciara were robbing people. I think if you tell her that you want to rob us, she will make it a personal mission, and that's how we're going to get her. She's going to want to rob us herself because we kicked her out on her ass."

"Okay, but she's going out of town tonight. So, we'll have to wait until she gets back," Tasha said, as she tossed her empty bag of chips into the garbage can.

"That's alright, because it will give us more time to set things up," Byron added.

Tasha chimed in, "Okay, let's do it. I'm ready for whatever."

******

The next day, Ciara arrived in Atlantic City with an attitude and money to spend.

"I don't understand why I can't pay with cash."

"Ma'am, because we only accept major credit cards at this hotel. Maybe you can try one that's further down the strip," the hotel clerk suggested.

"I'm not going anywhere! Look, how about I pay for my room and give you an extra hundred dollars every night I stay for your pockets?"

"No, I have to follow hotel policies," the gentleman replied.

"I have to follow hotel policies," Ciara repeated in a nerdy voice. "Whatever, dude," she said, then walked away with her

Louis Vuitton luggage.

As she reached the front of the hotel, her cell phone began to ring. It was Tasha.

"This hoe must be crazy. She has to be."

Ciara didn't bother to answer, sending Tasha to voicemail. About ten seconds later, when her phone alerted her that she had a message, she dialed her voicemail and entered 6-6-6-3-9, which spelled out the word money.

"Press one to listen to your messages," the automated voice instructed.

Ciara quickly pressed one.

"Hey, Ciara, it's Tasha. I'm sorry for everything. I was wrong for snapping at you like that the other day, but I just wanted to tell you to be safe and I'll see you when you come back. Oh yeah, I met this guy named Decorey, and I think we should make one last move. You know what I'm talking about, too. But call me back when you get a chance. Bye."

Ciara quickly dialed Tasha's number, and she picked up on the first ring.

"What's up, girl? I just called you," Tasha anxiously said after answering.

"I know. So what's up?"

"Well, first of all, I want to apologize for how I've been acting lately, and second, I have another job for us to do. I know I said I was done with the game, but this is going to be an easy lick to hit."

"Really? Who are we about to get?"

"I met this guy named Decorey, and he's balling out of control. He's fine and everything, but I just want to get his money. His brother was even trying to get at me on the low behind his back."

Tasha wasn't sure if Ciara was buying into her story, but she

Steven Morgan

knew she had her attention.

"But how do you know he has money?"

"Ciara, he spent about seventeen hundred dollars on me last night. I don't think a regular Joe Blow could do that type of spending."

"So? That still doesn't mean he has money up the ass. We are close to tax season, you know?"

"I know, Ciara, but I have a good feeling about this one. Besides, I need this money because I want to move."

"Move? You should have plenty of money to move with. Why do you want to move anyway?"

"I need to get out of Chicago. You always talk about moving to Georgia, and I'm not going to stay up here by myself waiting for some man to hopefully marry me someday. I'm trying to live life just like you."

"Why can't you just move with the money you have?"

"I can, but I want to leave my mother a nice stash before I get M.I.A."

This doesn't sound like the Tasha I know, Ciara thought. "Okay, I'm coming back on Saturday and we can talk about what we need to do then."

"Cool. Make sure you call me as soon as you make it into town."

"Okay, I will. Bye."

The coincidence of Tasha meeting Decorey was too good to be true. His brother coming on to her was a shock, because one thing Ciara knew about Byron was that he was a flaming homosexual that wouldn't dare get close to, or want, a woman. Ciara couldn't wait to get to the bottom of this. Tasha just sounded too eager to believe. Ciara had been in the game of setting people up long enough to get that feeling when she was being set up.

Two days later after, Ciara made it back into town, she and Tasha went to work on their plan. It didn't take long for the women to come up with the perfect way to rob Decorey and Byron.

"I promise, Ciara, this is the last time we're going to do this. It shouldn't be hard because we're not dealing with any hood niggas. These lames won't even see this one coming."

"Give me a couple of days and we can make it happen."

"Okay, but why in a couple of days?" Tasha pressed.

"I'm moving into this condo on Monday."

"Do you need help moving?"

"No, I'm cool, but I'll call you as soon as I'm finished with everything."

A couple of days went by, and Ciara was out of sight. Ciara threw a curve ball, and Tasha needed to connect with Decorey and Byron about the changes.

"What's up? When are we going to take care of this business?" Decorey frantically asked, while standing with Tasha at the agreed upon location.

"Soon, I'm just waiting to hear from Ciara. She hasn't been answering her phone, and the last time I talked to her, she said she was about to move into a condo."

"Good, I have a friend that can get me her new address."

"I don't want to rush anything, Decorey. I prefer for this to be done the right way."

"The right way?" he repeated. "Let me tell you something. This isn't going to take long, and it's not going to be hard. You just better be prepared for what we have in store for that bitch!" he told her, and pulled his shirt up, exposing the black handle of a gun.

"I'm ready. I just want things to go smoothly."

"It will. I want this bitch just as bad as you do."

About an hour later after going her separate way from Decorey, Tasha tried to call Ciara again. She was desperate for her to pick up this time.

The phone rang once and she answered.

"Who is this?" Ciara asked.

"Stop playing. It's me. Where have you been?"

"I told you that I had some running to do and I had to move."

"Yeah, but I didn't know you were going to take this long. We're supposed to take care of that business."

"Listen, I think I'm gonna have to pass on this one, Tasha."

Tasha's mouth dropped. "Why? What happened?" she quickly asked.

"I just have a bad feeling about the whole thing, and I think I should just follow my first mind."

"Wait a minute! You just can't back out on me like this, Ciara! Especially when I was counting on you to help me get this money."

"I know, but I just can't do it. It's not in me anymore to get down like that. I'm taking your advice and leaving this life of crime alone."

This bitch, Tasha thought. "Okay, I'm going to let you think about this some more, because I think you may be a little stressed out about moving and everything. So, get some sleep and call me back when you wake up!"

Click!

Tasha called Byron.

"Hello, this is the sweet and sexy Byron. How may I help

you, Miss Tasha?"

"She doesn't want to do it anymore, and I don't know if she's playing or what!" Tasha screamed into the phone.

"Calm down! Now what happened?"

"Ciara doesn't want to go along with the plan anymore! She said she doesn't want to live this life anymore and she wanted to basically walk a straight path."

"Why? What happened? Did you say anything to her that could've changed her mind?"

"She doesn't want to do it. What part of that don't you understand, Byron?"

"First of all, don't raise your voice at me, honey. Now, did you talk to Decorey yet?"

"No, I haven't talked to him yet. I'm sorry, Byron. I'm just nervous about everything right now."

"Well, don't worry about it. We'll figure this shit out. Damn, you got my blood pressure all up. I thought somebody died or something, girl," he said, while fanning himself with a *Black Enterprise* magazine. "Wait a minute. This is Decorey on the other end. I'll call you right back."

"Okay, tell me what he says," Tasha said before Byron clicked over to the other line.

"Hey, Decorey, I just got off the phone with Tasha and she told me that Ciara isn't cooperating."

"Don't worry about it because we're about to make a change in the plans ourselves. I just got Ciara's new address, and I think we should pay her a little visit tonight," Decorey whispered.

"For real? That's what I'm talking about, big bro. But what about, Tasha?"

"We'll leave Tasha out of this one. She'll thank us later for it. I have to go, but we will definitely take care of this later,"

Decorey said just before hanging up.

Later on that night, Tasha was excluded from the plans and the information. She hadn't heard from Byron, Decorey, or Ciara. She paced back and forth in her living room for about twenty minutes, and then her phone suddenly rang.

"Hello."

"Hey, it's me, and I can't really talk long, but Decorey is going to take care of you-know-who tonight."

"I can't hear you, Byron. Speak up."

"I can't talk loud because Decorey is here, but he's going to take care of the business himself tonight. Now, I have to go."

Byron quickly hung up the phone before Tasha could get out another word.

"Who was that on the phone?" Decorey asked, as he walked into the large family room where Byron was sitting.

"I was just checking my messages," he nervously replied, fumbling with the phone.

Decorey knew something was wrong because he could tell by the look on Byron's face.

"Okay, cool." Decorey sat down on the nearby couch.

"I'm about to run to the store real quick. Do you need anything?" Byron asked, as he grabbed his car keys.

"No, I'm cool. But why are you leaving now when you know we need to handle this business soon?"

"I just need to grab something for this headache before we go."

Decorey looked at Byron. He sensed he was telling a lie. He knew his brother too well.

"Just make it fast," Decorey replied.

As soon as Byron left out, Decorey got up and pressed redial on the house phone.

"Hello," Tasha answered in excitement. "Hello, Byron. I

can't hear you if you're saying something."

Decorey didn't say a word.

"Byron, why aren't you saying anything?"

Decorey hung up, sat back on the couch, and folded his hands while staring at the ceiling.

"What the hell was that about?" Tasha said. "First, Byron calls me talking all crazy, and then he calls back and doesn't say anything."

She grabbed her cell phone and dialed Ciara.

"Hello," Ciara said, answering after the fourth ring.

"Hey, it's me. I need a big favor from you, and please don't say no," Tasha begged.

"What is it? I'm kind of busy right now."

"I need you to hold my money for a couple of days. I think someone has been trying to break into my house. I just want you to hold it until I can deposit it into the bank. Please, Ciara, I need you just this one time."

"Okay, but where do you want me to meet you at?"

"Meet me at the Rock and Roll McDonald's downtown in fifteen minutes."

"Okay, I'm on my way."

Moments later, Tasha made it to McDonald's, and Ciara pulled in about two minutes afterwards. Tasha got out of her car and approached Ciara's car with two black book bags.

"I'm so glad you're doing this for me," she said after getting inside. "It's about sixty grand in each book bag. I don't care if you spend some, just don't leave me broke."

"It's cool, but is everything okay?"

"Everything will be cool," she said, then turned her head away from Ciara. "Just be sure to watch your back, Ciara. Just watch your back," she repeated.

Ciara knew something was wrong, but she couldn't pinpoint

the problem. Tasha gave Ciara a hug and quickly got out of the car. Before she got into her 300C, she looked back at Ciara, but didn't say anything. The two women looked at one another for a second and then went their separate ways.

Watch my back, huh? I think you need to watch yours, Ciara thought as she drove down busy Michigan Avenue.

On the drive back home, Tasha decided to check into a hotel room not too far from her place. She was nervous and paranoid. When she got the strange call from Byron she thought he had been setting her up this whole time. Once the sun came up in the morning, she was going to get her personal things and leave Chicago behind.

Chapter 21

"Stop fucking lying to me!" Decorey screamed at the half naked man lying in the bed shaking.

"Man, I'm telling you that you have the wrong person!" the man yelled, while trying to cover himself with the sheets.

"You think I'm stupid, motherfucker! I know Ciara Blackwell lives here! Where the fuck is that bitch?"

"I don't know what you're talking about. Listen, some years ago, I robbed this lady at the hotel, and me and my girl have been using her credit and identification. That's how we got this apartment. Please don't hurt me. I swear to God that I'm telling you the truth," the man pleaded.

Decorey pointed his fully loaded automatic towards Byron. "You knew about this shit, Byron?"

"No, what are you talking about?" Byron cried.

"Don't play with me. I'm talking about how you lied to me earlier about who was on the phone. I called the number back when you left and that bitch Tasha answered!" he shouted, waving the semi-automatic towards Byron.

"Calm down. I just told her that we were going to take care of everything ourselves. That's all. I wouldn't lie to you!"

"But you did lie! Just like you did when I asked were you dating Shawn behind my back."

"I'm sorry!" he said, reaching for Decorey's hand.

"I'm sorry, too, lil brother."

Decorey wiped a tear from his cheek and shot Byron in the head. Blood splattered across the room, and what was left of Byron's body fell to the floor with a lifeless thump. The thick blood gushed out onto the floor.

"Oh my God!" the man screamed from the bed.

Byron's body twitched and jerked as the last signs of the human being disappeared. The man was so scared that a yellow stain appeared on the light-colored sheets. The grown man pissed himself and was moments shy of shitting his pants.

Decorey turned to the man and shot him twice in the face. He then walked over to his brother's corpse and rubbed the right side of his face. The left cheek was almost completely shot off by the force of the bullet. Decorey would never be able to forgive himself for killing his brother, but he also couldn't let another day pass without punishing Byron for his betrayal.

Moments later, the sound of police sirens could be heard approaching the house. Decorey kissed Byron on the forehead and laid him back down on the floor carefully. Then he grabbed the gun off of the ground and placed the barrel inside his mouth.

God, forgive me for everything I've done.

As Decorey sat on the edge of the bed next to his other victim, he could hear the police banging on the door outside. He closed his eyes, and Byron's face was so vivid in his head that it seemed like his picture was on the inside of his eyelids. As one tear slowly rolled down his face, he pulled the trigger, and his body fell to the floor on top of Byron's.

******

The next morning, Tasha made it back to her house to gather some clothes and other small items. She was preparing to leave town in a hurry. As she rushed through her bedroom closet, someone rang the doorbell.

"Who the hell is that? I don't have time for any bullshit right now," Tasha said, as she placed her gym bag on the table. "Maybe it's Ciara with my money."

She ran down the stairs and grabbed a small kitchen knife out of the drawer. Then she slowly pulled back the curtains to see if she could see the person at the front door, but she couldn't.

"Who is it?" Tasha yelled.

When no one answered, she quickly swung open the door, but she didn't see anyone. As soon as she went to close the door back, a man jumped from behind the bushes and threw battery acid in her face. She fell to the ground screaming and kicking. The man dropped the metal container and ran. Tasha's screams became ear piercing.

"Help me! It hurts!"

She was lying in her doorway shaking and holding her face. Just from her screams alone, one could imagine the pain she suffered. The tattered looking man continued to run until he reached a nearby alley about three blocks from her house.

"Okay, I did it. Can I get my money now?" the crackhead asked.

Ciara reached into the backseat and pulled five one-hundred-dollar bills from the black book bag.

"Good doing business with you," the fiend said, as he took the money, drooling over the amount of rocks he could buy for the next few days.

She zipped the bag closed and grabbed the strawberry cigarillo that was drying on the dashboard. She looked at herself in the rearview mirror and smiled. Her anthem was playing, so she turned up the volume to blast Young Jeezy and R. Kelly's

Steven Morgan

"Go Getta" before pulling out of the alley.

As the next part of her plan, Ciara pulled up in front of Tasha's house and saw a crowd of people surrounding her. She got out of the car and walked over to the crowd with the blunt still in her hand.

"I don't know what happened," the old lady said. "She's so sweet. Why would anyone want to hurt her?"

"Well, somebody didn't think she was so sweet," replied one young man who was sitting on his bike.

The sound of help arriving grew closer and louder. The ambulance and police finally arrived and cleared everyone away from the scene so they could tend to Tasha's injuries. The combination of the acid and her skin left a sour and unforgettable smell in the air. The paramedics hoisted Tasha and carefully placed her into the ambulance. Ciara watched from a short distant as everything took place.

Ciara warned Tasha that she had nothing to lose, and this was her way of showing Tasha who really was the boss bitch. Ciara incurred too many disappointments and setbacks in her life to allow Tasha to manipulate or try to outplay her. She moved a strand of hair out of her face and put her Prada sunglasses over her eyes. This was Ciara's farewell to Tasha and their short, tumultuous partnership.

Ciara got back into her car and headed towards the BP gas station up the street. She was standing in front of the bulletproof window asking for a fill-up on pump six and a lighter, when a guy spoke to her from behind the counter.

"Damn, baby girl, I think I know you from somewhere," the gas attendant said.

"I'm not from around here, sorry."

Ciara grabbed her money and left the store.

"I know that bitch from somewhere," he repeated. "Hey,

watch the counter, Melvin. I have to make a quick phone call."

"Hurry up, Marco. I'm about to take my break," the gas station worker replied.

Marco grabbed his cell phone and walked out of the gas station.

Damn! Damn! Damn! That's the nigga Tasha stole the ounce of weed from on Kilpatrick. Shit! I'll just get gas somewhere else, Ciara thought, then quickly jumped into her car.

"Yeah, I know it's that bitch now, because she's pulling off and she didn't even pump her gas. Her and that fat-ass bitch Tasha took some weed from me when I was working for Big Lord," Marco said, watching Ciara's every move.

"I'm right here about to turn into the gas station now, Marco. What kind of car is she in?" the male on the other end of the phone asked.

"She's in that Range Rover right there." Marco pointed in the direction Ciara drove her car.

"Oh, I see her. Let me take care of this."

The man on the phone hung up and grabbed his gun off of the passenger seat.

Ciara pulled out of the gas station burning rubber. She looked in the rearview mirror to see a green Monte Carlo approaching her. The car was gaining speed on her, and she gripped the steering wheel tighter. She and Tasha had played so many people in Chicago that it could have been just about anyone coming after her.

The car continued to follow Ciara as they raced through traffic lights and down narrow one-way streets. When the Monte Carlo came up close on her, the driver cocked his all-black automatic weapon and let off three shots at Ciara's Range Rover.

Steven Morgan

     "What the fuck! He's shooting at me! Please, God, help me. I don't deserve this!"

     The first shot missed, but the second and third were dead on. The shot shattered the back window, hitting Ciara in the left shoulder. The man shot two more times before speeding away down a side street.

     Ciara felt the burning sensation creeping down her arm and through the rest of her petite body. As she lost control of the car, it went across the opposite lane and rammed head-on into a large U-Haul truck.

     The impact was sudden and powerful. Ciara was instantly thrown out of the front windshield. Her left leg was mangled under her body and blood poured from the back of her head. Her left arm was split open from her elbow to her wrist, exposing her bone. The cold concrete and blood was the only thing Ciara could feel as everything became blurry.

     "Please call 9-1-1! Ma'am, stay calm. Help is on the way," a helpful witness said, as he tried to prop Ciara's body into a comfortable position.

     Ciara's eyes were flickering, and her right arm was shaking. By the time the ambulance arrived, she wasn't moving.

     "I think we're losing her!" the medic screamed.

     "No! Please, Ciara, stay with us! Come on, not another one today, guys! Keep fighting! I'm right here with you!" a nervous medic cried.

     Ciara couldn't hear anything that was going on around her. She began to see flashes of herself when she was a little girl playing with Kim in the streets. She then saw her and Shawn on their wedding day. As the medics tried their best to save her, one medic looked down and noticed a slight smile on her face. After all of the hurt and pain she went through, it's like she finally accepted what her life had become. The visions of Kim and Shawn left her mind and everything faded to black. Ciara's smile was gone and her twitching stopped.

Everyone standing around the scene was speechless as one medic got up, walked over to the curb, and sat down. He was covered with Ciara's blood and his hands were trembling uncontrollably.

"Everything's going to be okay. This is the hardest part of this job. It still bothers me as well when I lose one, Eric," the medic said, as he patted his coworker on the back.

"One of my closest friends died on this same street. Almost in the same exact spot, too. It's so crazy, because her best friend was this woman right here," Eric said, while looking at Ciara lying on the ground with a white sheet covering her body.

"Really? Who is she?" the medic sadly asked.

Eric took a deep breath.

"This is my brother Shawn's widow….Ciara Blackwell!"